The Elizabeths

Judith Nichols Mowery

This book is a novel of fiction. Any resemblence to persons and places are purely coincidence..

Copyright © 2012 Judith Nichols Mowery
All rights reserved.

ISBN: 1470077434
ISBN 13: 9781470077433

Library of Congress Control Number: 2012902908
CreateSpace, North Charleston, SC

CHAPTER ONE

JUNE 1st

LIZ

LIZ hears the airplane before she sees it and runs across the hard-packed sand to the line of foam left by the last wave. As the roar of the plane's engine grows louder she races north as if trying to outrun her pursuer. Suddenly she stops and whirls around to face the small plane as it skims the nearby waves. Inside the cockpit her husband Peter flashes a wide smile as he tips the wings in a quick salute then banks the plane to the northeast to soar up over the coastal mountain range straight into the rising sun. Waving and blowing kisses Liz laughs with delight. She loves this early morning race that sends Peter off to his marketing company near Boeing Field. Running her fingers through her short mop of white hair Liz watches the plane disappear over the near peaks and whispers, "Fly safe, my love, take care."

Stretching before resuming her run to the north cliffs Liz sees more people on the south beach yet the three mile stretch of beach north to the red cliffs is empty. Happy to have the beach to herself she decides to make her own race to the slab of rock lying at the cliff's base and is running at full speed when something hits her hard on her right shoulder causing her to stumble forward until her hands touch down leaving prints in the sand.

"I'm so sorry," she calls out as she rights herself. Looking to where she is certain another person will be and is surprised when no one is there. "That's strange I would swear someone ran into me," she muses as she studies her handprints in the sand and one lone footprint ahead of them. Chuckling at the sight she must have been she tries to fit fingers and foot into the prints at the same time and can not. "What kind of wild dance did I do to get my foot that far ahead of me?" As if in reply a large grey gull sweeps past her landing near a pile of flotsam and begins to peck amongst it. "So you're the culprit," she laughs as she resumes her run.

When she reaches the cliffs and steps onto the huge slab of red rock Liz slaps the roundish stone protruding from the cliff face and shouts, "I declare this run good and done!" Turning to look at the beach to the south she studies the row of houses between the deep sand dunes and the one road which winds its way up to the State Park at the top of the red cliffs Shoreline Drive. These homes are owned by year-round residents and protected from harsh winter storms by the cliffs and sea grass topped dunes. Her own home sits on the highest point three miles south on the wooded five acres where her father built his small cabin when she was a child. The original cabin was remodeled by Peter into a comfortable home when they decided to move here thirty years ago.

Liz leans against the cool cliff face and feels her legs tingle from the run. "Whew old girl you don't have to set a record every run." She tells herself chuckling, 'It's hard not to try though. This run is my connection with Dana. I raced her to this rock whenever our folks brought us to the beach. Each of us had to be first to slap our touchstone. I miss her and our folks so much. Damn that drunk driver who crashed into us and killed them all."

Lifting her eyes Liz watches seabirds drop off cliffs overhead then soar out to sea. Suddenly a bright light flashes into her eyes causing her to close them for several seconds. Opening them she sees a green imprint of an object crossing the scene before her. By the time it fades the sun cracks the sky over the mountain tops coloring the clouds on the western horizon brilliant pinks and oranges. With the sunrise comes a mountain-cooled wind chasing a thick fog onto the beach. Shorebirds scream excitedly as the clouds reflecting the sunrise color the dunes rusts and purples. As the fog thickens Liz watches the colors fade blurring the line between waves and sky.

"Damn. That fog must have filled the canyons in the mountains. Peter hates flying through fog using instruments. It must have been hell going over Mt. Michael." Checking her watch she notes that it's almost seven. "He should be at Boeing Field by now. I'm sure he'll tell me all about it when he calls later. Hopefully he and Bob Drake can finalize the sale of their company today."

As the fog slowly wipes the beach from her sight a sudden chill runs over her and she rubs her arms. "Good thing Peter put up that flagpole at the entrance of our path through the dunes so I wouldn't get lost. I'm going to need it this morning." Just then a wind gust pushes the fog aside long enough for her to see down the beach to where the flag snaps its brilliance in a shot of sunlight and the sight fills Liz with gratitude and love.

The trip home is much slower as the fog becomes so thick she needs to follow the edge of the waves. Beachcombers, joggers, and families pop in and out of the gray as she nears them making the trek almost an adventure. Sounds of children's laughter and barking dogs intermingle with the cries of shorebirds creating a sort of overture. Once in a while she recognizes a face and waves to the person. Only when she hears the familiar snapping of the flag in the wind does she realize she is at the flagpole near the path to her home and she turns from the waves to follow the sound.

Through the mist she sees a tall dark woman standing at the entrance of the path through the dunes and Liz waves to her neighbor to the north Alexandra Petrow. As she walks to the woman she smiles and knows that Alex is her friend more than Peter's. To him she is 'Radcliff's Raunchy Russian Royalty with a twisted vodka accent.' Once Alex heard him and laughed telling him it was truer than he'd guess. During the long winter evening in front of one fireplace or another Alex's stories entertained and delighted the year-round residents of Redcliffs. As her story goes she trained for the Russian ballet and defected to the West in her late twenties to never dance again. It was then that she moved to this secluded community to hone her clairvoyant abilities which she claims get her high fees for readings of others' futures.

When she reaches Alex, Liz braces for the hug she knows is coming. "Hey-lo, Liz, Hey-lo!" the tall woman shouts as she wraps her arms around Liz. "How you?" Alexandria asks as she releases Liz. "Saw you fellow took off. You like talk? Need catch up? OK? Come; I cook. Grate beets to fry make Mama's yummy pot stickers. OK?"

Liz nods as she answers, "Hi Alex. It's wonderful to have you home again and I'm starving so yes to your pot stickers. I have an article to finish but it can wait. I write better at night when Peter's away. He and Bob Drake are negotiating the sale of their company and he may have to stay in Seattle until it's completed. Peter says it's time for him to retire and I agree."

"Oh is so Liz? See changes. Yah. See Peter much change. He make change for you too? You see?" Alex smiles as she takes Liz's hand.

Frowning Liz pulls her hand away. "No Alex I don't see. Why do you always have to tell me something about Peter?" Shaking her head she tries to put her image of her life back where it had been a moment ago. "Do you hear me Alex? I've told you before that I don't want you to tell my future. Whatever is to be will happen without your saying so."

Alex's smile crumples. "Liz is no-ting. Peter go. Not mean upset you."

"Well you did. I just told you Peter will be in Seattle for a few days. Of course there'll be changes when Peter sells the company, we plan to travel a lot together. I'll stay on as editor for *Travel Tips Magazine* a few more months. However Peter's future is his to decide himself." Liz's expression softens. "Now it's your turn to tell all Alex. Where did you go last week? The whole beach gang is speculating on what you do when you rush off like that. You know how we enjoy your intriguing tales. Did you meet with someone special this time?"

"See many persons." Alex stops then stares intently into Liz's eyes. "You hear Liz. Most exciting happens. You run beach to north cliffs woman runs with you. You wave Peter flews by. Woman run past. No she go through you. You fall. She run to rock. You run too. Then step up. Both slap rock same time. You turn face here. Woman to waves pick thing up. Big wave sweep woman cross rock." Alex stares into Liz's eyes. "She go through you. Yah, she do, Liz. Not by side. No. She go through you. She fall on sand. Sit at stump. Then walk wit you here. I shout Hey-lo. Poof she go." Alex snaps her fingers. "She you wit hair-tail. You shine gold together. Yah it true. Liz you gold. You see? It amazes. Liz. Is wonder. Wonder. Am sorry shout hey-lo. You not see woman?"

Liz stares at Alex. She doesn't move or speak. Only her eyes look to where she knows the red cliffs are three miles north behind the thick fog. Her mind's eye sees the ancient log sunk deep into the high dry sand. Her mouth opens and closes as her tongue tries to form the words stuck in her throat. She shakes her head as if to understand what Alex has seen.

Finally Liz manages to whisper, "Alex what do you mean you saw this person? There was no one with me near the cliffs. Then the fog got so thick by the time I started home I couldn't see more than a few feet in front of me. On the way up I did stumble after Peter's flyby. You saw me do that right? I left prints in the sand near the wave line. At the rock sunlight flashed into my eyes blinding me for several seconds and I had to close them. That's what it was Alex. Don't you see? It was the sun coming over the mountains."

Even as she protests to Alex goose bumps cover Liz's arms. She can feel her scalp rise as she stares into the fog trying to see the base of the cliffs. Slowly she turns to Alex and asks, "Is she here? Do you see her now? Could it be Dana? I thought so much about her this morning. You know she died years ago in the same accident that killed our parents. Alex it would be wonderful if it were her. Why would she come to me at this time? What could it mean? Can you see her now? Tell me all you saw."

Alex's face softens yet she shakes her head. "Too many peoples now. No see thing. Come we cook. Talk. Eat good foods. Alex love fix foods." As usual Alex manages to turn Liz's concerns aside as she guides her. Letting herself be led up the path to the steps to Alex's home Liz wonders for a brief moment, *Will Alex tell me where she went last week?*

It is nearly four in the afternoon when the two women say their good-byes and Liz walks the path through the wooded acreage her father bought years ago and still shields her home from the busy traffic on Shoreline Drive. At the high point on the trail Liz stops to lean against an ancient storm-twisted tree. On the beach below the dunes she sees the sun has burned off much of the fog.

"If Dana had survived the accident she would have built her cabin exactly where I'm standing now," Liz realizes with a rush of sadness. A shiver crosses her shoulders as the breeze wraps its chill around her bringing with it sounds from the beach. In them she thinks she hears her name being called and she hurries down the last stretch of path to her driveway. When she emerges from the high bush she is surprised to see a sheriff's car parked in front of the garage. A tall uniformed man is walking from the front door towards the north side deck.

Frightened Liz shouts at him, "Hello? Hello? Can I help you? Are you looking for someone? Can I help you?"

At the sound of her voice the deputy waves to her and walks up the driveway to meet her. "Hello? Are you Mrs. Day? I'm looking for Mrs. Peter Day. Would that be you?"

"Yes I'm Mrs. Peter Day. Liz Day. How can I help you?" She pants the words hoping he will not answer. More than anything else she does not want to hear what he has to say.

"Mrs. Day? Can we go inside your home before we talk? Please? Let me take you inside. Is this the best way?" As he speaks he gently takes her arm and leads her to the front door of her home. "Can you open the door for us? Let's go inside where we can talk privately."

Without answering Liz unlocks the door. Once inside she rushes through her home to the wide bank of windows facing the ocean. The deputy steps up behind her and gently touches her arm. He is too gentle as he guides her to the closest chair, Peter's chair, and gently eases her into it.

Kneeling in front of her he speaks softly. "Mrs. Day I have very bad news. Your husband's plane crashed this morning. It seems he flew too low in the fog and crashed into the highest mountain north of here, Mt. Michael. Reports from witnesses say they heard a small plane having engine trouble around six this morning. Said it was very low. That's all just too low. Then the engine stopped and the plane crashed. We got several reports of the crash. However due to a thick fog it took most of the morning to locate the crash site. Luckily the locator in his plane turned on, on impact. Rescue crews had to go by foot as helicopters couldn't go up in that fog.

"Mrs. Day? Are you listening to me? Mrs. Day? I'm sorry to have to tell you this. Is there anything I can get you? Anyone I could call for you? Mrs. Day?"

CHAPTER TWO

June 1st

BETH

BETH watches the waves roll across the sand knowing they will touch the uprights under her cabin's deck before they flow back into the next wave. She grasps the railing of the hospital bed which dominates the one main room of the cabin and stares silently out the sliding glass doors. When her father bought the acreage this was the highest point on the beach and he built the cabin as if it were a yacht making cabinets, windows and doors to hold against the strongest storms. Beth remembers being a small child when the family first began coming summer after summer always sure their cabin would be waiting for them. In the beginning rows of cabins sat south of the cliffs hidden behind massive sea grass covered dunes daring the ocean's furies to come closer. Then for years storms with demon waves battered both cabins and high dunes until even the gentlest winds seemed to sweep away the last bits of both. Now the only cabin standing along Redcliff's Beach is her own and the high sand dunes are nearly flattened.

A soft moan from the body on the hospital bed brings Beth back to the present. Turning slowly she studies the emaciated woman lying under the bedding and watches each shallow breath taken. Kissing the cool cheek nearest her Beth whispers, "That's right my love breathe darling Maxine. Breathe release breathe release."

Holding one thin hand in both of hers she presses it to her lips and prays, "Please Lord let this be a good day a day without pain a day without fear. Let her sleep be undisturbed. Give her a day of peace." As she tucks the cool hand under the blanket Beth whispers, "I'll be back soon my love. I'm going for our run to the cliffs. Sleep. I'll be back soon."

Knowing not to expect an answer she picks a hooded sweatshirt off the nearby chair and puts it on. Quietly she opens the slider door and slips onto the deck closing the door behind her. Ignoring the steps down to the beach she leaps to the sand running as soon as she lands. Without slowing she races along the wave line toward the red cliffs three miles ahead.

Inside the cabin beloved eyes open at the sound of the closing door. Starkly beautiful black eyes watch Beth's escape as blue-tinged lips smile their understanding. Maxine wakens from feigned sleep to again join Beth's morning run and wills her essence out to the beach. She feels the memory of feet smacking wet sand feels cold water wash over bare feet and feels the joy of running free with feet pounding in tandem. Maxine soars over the waves to the tops of the cliffs then settles deep into Beth's heart.

Beth feels this every time she leaves the cabin for her run. Though Maxine cannot be seen Beth knows her love is with her willing herself to run matching stride for stride as she did for over thirty years. Beth pushes hard leaving deep footprints at the edge of the wet sand and wishes there were two sets instead of just hers.

Leaping over a seaweed-wrapped float log Beth feels a strong bump on her left side. As she turns to see what she hit a large gull flies past. Laughing she calls out to the large bird, "Sorry! I wasn't in the mood to run around that heap back there. See you at the cliffs." The Gull gives a cry as it flaps slowly ahead as if leading her to the slab of red rock at the base of the high cliffs.

As her feet pound the hard sand Beth wants more than anything else in the world to live her life with Maxine over again. She wishes the day longer and the end nowhere in sight. She wants those wonderful years filled with joy and laughter all over again. Beth knows she must remember the good years and not dwell on these past years. "Max asked me to let her go. I didn't answer her as she is halfway there. I see it in her eyes with each breath she takes. The struggle is over. She no longer fights to live. She wants to leave this life."

Tears blur Beth's vision as she nears the cliffs. Her heart pounds in her ears and she chants with each step, "One, more, day, please, dear, God; one, more, day. I, have, nothing, nothing, left, after, all, the, promises, made; each, day, this, year, this, week. I, gave, her, all. I have, nothing, left, to, give, just, love."

Finally Beth steps onto the huge slab of stone that cracked off the steep red cliffs eons before. Feeling its cool wave-smoothed surface beneath her bare feet she slaps at the round protruding red stone in the cliff face and declares, "This run is good and done." Tears roll down her cheeks as she looks out at the ocean and whispers, "Max how can I survive without you? You are my darling my soul. How will I live without your laughter?"

Through her tears she sees a flash of bright pink within a wave as it sweeps up to the base of the rock. Blinking her tears away she sees it is a large snail shell. For several seconds she stares at it in wonder. Only when the shell begins to retreat with the wave does Beth jump into the water and capture it. It is empty and completely unmarred. She holds it up to catch the sunlight and marvels, "What a beauty you are. I've never seen a shell so large or brightly colored on this beach. You're empty so you can't have just fallen off the cliffs. Maybe there are more of you around the point."

Tucking the shell into a pocket of her sweatshirt she wades into the waves to look along the bottom of the cliff face. As she studies the cliff's bottom edge a sudden high wave swirls up over her knees and pushes her backward nearly floating her onto the rock slab. While she catches her balance a brilliant light blinds her for several seconds. As she blinks her eyes to clear the flash imprint another wave washes over the rock and pushes her off the other side onto hard packed sand where she stumbles and falls onto her knees.

Shaken Beth limps up to an ancient hollow tree trunk poking high out of dry sand. Sitting next to it she rubs her tender knees while remembering when this had been a place where she and her sister played dolls. At that time the dunes were high and filled the tree's hollow trunk to the top leaving only a few feet of the silvered wood making a sort of child's play house. Now years later the waves have sucked the sand from its hollow form letting the silvered monolith show its full weathered elegance. Years before her father told her that when he was a child there had been a cedar forest stretching westward for over a mile along this very beach. Even at that time several ancient tree trunks showed themselves further out during the lowest tides. These signs of beach erosion were the main reason her father built the cabin with his shipbuilding skills.

Letting her thoughts wander back to summer mornings when she raced her sister Dana each wanting to be the first to slap the touchstone and yell, "I declare the run good and done." Beth whispers, "Redcliff's Beach you are my past, my present, and hopefully my future. You hold my touchstone in your red cliffs."

BETH

When a strong gust of wind tugs at her ponytail sending one long white strand dancing above her head Beth shivers chilled by the cooling dampness of her jeans. Pushing herself to her feet an odd sort of longing comes over her. The beach is empty. No one else is on the full seven miles of shoreline. Waves roll across the flat three miles of sand between her and where the cabin sits. Beth sees that they come closer to the base of the cabin then they did last summer. "Please let the cabin stay safe while Max lives," she whispers. "After that you can do whatever must be."

Brushing the sand off her damp clothes her hand hits the hard bulk of the pink shell in her sweatshirt pocket and she takes it out to study it one more time before zipping it back inside the pocket. "It's a perfect shell for my perfect Maxine."

The run back to the cabin is slow as her knees hurt from the fall onto the sand. She wants to scream Maxine's name with every step. Instead she runs against the silent fear that sends her home wherever she goes, the fear that what she left might be no more. When she reaches the cabin she bounds across the deck and opens the slider door. Seeing the still shape under the bedding on the hospital bed she closes the door and holds her breath against the room's silence. Then she sees Maxine's eyes open and Beth breathes again.

Though she barely lifts her head Max takes the shell Beth hands her. Seeing her weakness Beth shivers and very gently tucks both shell and Maxine's hand under the blanket. At that moment Maxine closes her eyes to slip away to that place she resides more now than with Beth. Leaning over her love Beth kisses the cool forehead whispering, "The beautiful shell is for you my darling. It's a gift from the ocean to my dear Maxine."

Suddenly Maxine's eyes open wide as she pulls the shell from under the blanket. "So lovely. Where?" Her too-bright eyes watch Beth's face as she hears the story. At the end a smile crosses her lips. "Beth darling…must go…shell holds my love always."

Beth swallows hard as she fights back her tears. "I will cherish it always my darling. I will tell everyone it's a gift from the most wonderful amazing loving beautiful woman my soul mate my best friend my love my Maxine." Taking a deep breath Beth gulps back a sob. "Did you see the sun is out today? When it warms up later we'll sit on the deck. Would you like that?"

Though Beth forces lightness in her voice she sees Maxine has closed her eyes and struggles for breathes. She whispers, "Where do you go my darling? Are loved ones waiting to greet you? Is that why you go so often? Is it somewhere wonderful?"

As if an answer the pink shell rolls out of Maxine's hand onto the sheet. Beth picks it up and holds it up to the sunlight. "What a beauty you are. Such beauty at a time I need it so. How lucky I was to find you. How lucky I was to have found Maxine. You come into my life as Maxine did, both of you perfectly amazingly wonderful."

While Maxine sleeps Beth sits beside the bed holding the shell in one hand and Maxine's hand with her other. When Max wakes she tells Beth her dream of sailing on a deep blue sea in a pink shell boat searching for Beth. A joyous love beams from her eyes. "I found you here as always." As Beth leans in to kiss Maxine's forehead the black eyes close and Maxine sleeps again.

Going to the dining table Beth places the shell on a plate of shells sitting in the center of the table. Picking up her coffee mug and cereal bowl left over from breakfast she rinses them in the sink. Then she pours the leftover coffee from the carafe and heats it in the microwave. As she returns with the hot coffee mug Max is still in a deep sleep. Reaching to set the mug on the bedside table Beth bumps it on the edge and some hot coffee sloshes onto her hand. "Damn that's hot!" she yelps.

BETH

Hurrying back to the kitchen sink she runs cold water over the reddening skin and memories flood her mind causing her to laugh softly. Beth returns to the sleeping woman and whispers, "Maxine remember how you demanded whenever I had a cup of coffee I say 'I like my coffee just as I like my women, hot and black.' You told me I to say that whenever we had coffee wherever we were. 'It'll lighten the mood in a manner of speaking,' you'd laugh. 'After all we're two powerful women and others have to know we can laugh at ourselves. We've certainly shaken up our section of the world being lesbians, ebony and ivory, with framed PhDs hanging on our walls so full of ourselves and to hell with what others think.' How lucky I was to have found you Maxine. Years ago we joined our lives together on this beach in front of and blessed by loving friends and family. Each of us stood before God and declared our love for the other. And it's lasted thirty years come this Sunday. What a miracle of love we are." Beth tells the sleeping woman on the bed then kisses the cool cheek closest to her.

Smiling sadly she takes the coffee-mug out the slider and crosses to the deck railing to study the empty seven-mile stretch of Redcliff's Beach. The wind is brisk and strong gusts whip high rollers across the sand leaving lines of foam along the row of cement uprights under the decking where she stands. Flecks of foam sail past shorebirds pecking into flotsam at the edge of the waves. Beth feels desperately alone as she realizes the future without Maxine is too close to measure.

Her thoughts go again to her childhood and the family that loved her and wished her sister Dana and she could be friends as they were before the accident. Dana was the only one hurt because she refused to use her seatbelt as it wrinkled her blouse. Years later when their folks died they left the cabin to both sisters hoping they would become close again. Dana didn't want anything to do with the cabin or Beth and Maxine. She said the place was a piece of junk and wouldn't be tied to it or the queers who lived in it. She wanted her share in cold cash. So

Max and Beth got a loan and paid her off. Dana laughed when she took the money saying they were fools as the place would fall into the sea just as the other cabins had. Beth laughed, "Well the joke's on her. It's still standing."

Then she muses, "If only it stays standing while Max lives. The sea can have it after she goes for all I care. I can see it's only hanging on by those steel beams. If those hadn't been in place last winter the cabin would have washed away in one of those pounding storms. Max and I rode them out with the floorboards shaking so hard our teeth rattled. Then a week later her doctors wrote that her tests showed Max's cancer was terminal and she had only a few months to live. That was when I decided to turn the cabin and land back to the State of Washington to be a shoreline preserve named in Max's honor. The decision was easy and Maxine was thrilled. The state agency agreed the land would have no further development and named it 'The Maxine Oakley Preserve'. Though she was ill Max went to sign the papers. The final transfer of the title pleased everyone except Dana who when she heard what I'd done demanded the cabin be transferred to her twins Nicole and Nancy even though she was told the cabin belongs to the State.

Last week Dana's husband Ed called to warn us to keep our doors locked as Dana was again off her meds and threatening us. He said the twins were moving to their own places and he was leaving as soon as they did. Beth heard the sadness in his voice and realized the situation was bad so she contacted her lawyer who got an injunction banning Dana from within a mile of Redcliff's Beach.

Maxine cried with relief, 'My life is too near the end. I'm tired of fighting your damned cancer of a sister and this damned cancer within me. You're the only thing that matters. I'm done. Life's too much of a struggle. I feel horrific all of the time every minute of every day all day and most of all I'm tired of fighting for every damned breath.'

BETH

Beth knows now it will be over soon. She could no longer pretend she didn't see death in Max's eyes and smell death surrounding them both. Last week Beth was too afraid she would lose Max. Now she prays Maxine passes quickly while she sleeps. Not holding on one more second. Not enduring one more painful day. She wants peace for them both and no more pain.

Noticing the horizon is darkening Beth growls, "Hell. Here comes another storm. I'd better get candles out." As she turns to cross to the glass slider door Beth feels a change in the air and is startled to see the slider door replaced by a set of French doors. A feeling of panic overwhelms her and she blinks trying to change what she sees. Then a woman with shoulder-length white hair crosses in front of her and opens one of the French doors. Completely frightened Beth calls out, "Hey what do you think you're doing? Stop right there. Did you hear me? Stop right there!"

Oblivious to Beth the woman continues through the French door and closes it behind her. Stunned Beth stammers, "What the hell? Where do you think you are going?" Rushing through her slider door and past the hospital bed she is dumbfounded to see the woman open a tall door at the end of a long hallway. Then without a backward glance the woman steps out the door and closes it behind her. "Stop right there." Beth screams at the woman as the door closes.

At that moment the carved doors vanish and Beth finds herself inside her own bathroom at the end of her cabin's hallway. Turning around she runs to the cabin's entry door which opens into her carport. When she is outside she searches for the woman and finds no one.

Puzzled Beth goes back into the cabin. As she shuts the door a deep groan brings Beth rushing to the hospital bed where Maxine is tugging at the bedding and moaning loudly. "No more. No more. Beth need Beth darling where?"

"I'm here Max. I'm right here." Beth chokes as she gathers Maxine's emaciated body in her arms and whispers. "I'm here my love I'm here."

Suddenly Maxine's eyes open wide and she gasps as a radiant smile moves across her face. "Beth it's so wonderful."

"I love you Maxine." Beth whispers even though she knows the love of her life, her Maxine is gone.

CHAPTER THREE

JUNE 1st

ELIZA

ELIZA wakens early this first morning after spending her first night in her newly rebuilt home and looks out the easterly windows to see gulls backlit by the rising sun soar up to the top of the house. "My God it's so good to wake up in this perfect room in my perfect home at my perfect Redcliff's Beach and it looks as if the gulls are enjoying the peak of the widow's walk. I'm so glad I insisted we add that to the plan. It's going to be a great place to spend summer evenings and winter days. That idiot Jack thought I was simply adding a room or two to Dad's old cabin. Did he really think I'd retire and move to something like that? What a laugh."

Snuggling under the quilt the memory of yesterday's festivities brings a smile to her face. The party was hosted by her ex-husband Jack Staples who everyone expected would be named her replacement that same day. Of course the fact that she holds all the voting stock in the company and the Board will follow her suggestion as to who her replacement should be probably didn't have anything to do with his being so personable for the day. He gave a nice speech after the dinner then handed her keys to a new BMW. She tried to act surprised and thanked him even though she was the one who signed the check for it. Then Eliza gave each employee a personal bonus gift from her for work well done. Finally Eliza explained that Jack being chosen to replace her was his mother Minna Staples' last wish. She quoted Minna saying 'Jack should step into the position with eagerness, maturity and finesse.' That said Eliza turned to the Chairman of the Board and gave him her keys to the company showing to all who would be in control. Then the Chairman handed the keys to Jack announcing he was the Boards selection to head the company. Jack was so pleased he kissed both cheeks of Eliza and the Chairman of the Board then took several bows to the applause of the employees.

"I'm done with the company and that asshole Jack. I gave thirty years to him and twenty to the company. It's wonderful to be done with both. Jack and I haven't spoken more than twenty words a day for the past twenty years. I was more alone at the Staples Mansion towering over the great Columbia River than I ever will be here at Redcliff's Beach. My decision to remodel Dad's old cabin and move here full time was the best thing I've ever done. Now the house is done. Both Dana's and my suites are completely finished and mine is furnished beautifully as are the common rooms on the first floor. There's still a bit to do on the smaller lower level suites for Dana's twins Julia and Janice but Dana can do those after she moves here.

"What a great friend she's been to me. When I finally had enough with Jack's screwing anything with boobs that walked upright, Dana supported my decision to divorce him and then encouraged me to stay at the Mansion with his mother Minna until she passed away. Dana was the one of us lucky in love. Her husband Jim was a good kind person. His death last winter was a shock for her and the twins. Now she's going to make her new life here rather than stay in Hood River."

When the memories continue to come at her, Eliza hurries into her spacious bathroom and turns on the shower. She feels as if she needs to clean off whatever crud was left by staying in the same house with Jack as long as she did. As she's scrubbing herself she shouts, "To hell with him. He's the same shit his father Mel was. Nothing pleased either of them. Thank God his mother Minna was my friend and encouraged me to spend my summers here. Finally she came with me and bought the Jeep so we could drive up and down the beach. It was Minna who named the Jeep Charlie. She told her friends in Hood River that Charlie gave a good ride when we were here at Redcliff's. It drove Mel crazy to hear her say that. I'll drive Charlie while I'm here and keep the new Beamer for trips to Portland. No sense exposing that beautiful car to salt air any more than necessary."

Once dressed Eliza grabs her keys and heads into the garage. After tucking her purse under the passenger seat of the Jeep she looks at the shiny BMW. The two contrasting images make her smile. "It's OK, Charlie," she tells the Jeep as she turns the key in the starter. "You're my main man at Redcliff's as long as you can get up and go."

She backs the Jeep slowly up the drive as she waits for the garage door to close. Elation fills Eliza as she marvels at the look of her new home. The widow's walk is the full third level and sits high above neighboring roofs. The home covers half of the acre her mom kept after her dad's death. Wide eaves rap the house covering decks on every side. Large banks of windows look both west and north with high venting windows on the south and east sides. Wide front steps sweep up to a broad stoop where a set of ten-foot high carved doors with stained glass sidelights tucks under the deep eave in the exact center of the house.

"What wonderful work the builder did on this house. It's as amazing outside as it is inside. Every room is bigger than the folks' whole cabin had been and I needed that widow's walk as a symbol of kicking Jack out of my life. Besides I don't want anyone sneaking up on me." Laughing Eliza turns the Jeep around in the wide driveway and pulls onto Shoreline Drive. "I wanted modern prairie style and got it. Don't think I could stand one more antique after living in the Staples Mansion all those years. This time it is all white leather, ebony woods and marble."

As she drives the Jeep down the road she sees her neighbors Al and Penny Goodwin at the top of their drive waving her down. "Hello Eliza. We saw you come in yesterday. It's good to have you back at the beach. The tides are great this week. In fact the next low is a minus eight at two thirty this afternoon. Will we see you out on the beach?"

"Good to see you both again. No beach for me today. I have so much to do in the house. You do know I'm here for good this time? Left Jack to take care of his own messes."

"Then it's even better than we thought," laughs Penny. "We all love you yet dreaded the times Jack came. I'm having some of the gang over for dinner tomorrow night. Could you make it?"

"Wonderful. I'll bring dessert," Eliza agrees. "See you then."

Further down Shoreline Drive she sees many new cabins amongst the wind-twisted evergreens along the high side of the road. Halfway to town there is a new casino in the last stages of completion. When the road drops close to the beach she sees vehicles racing the long stretch of wet-packed sand.

"Look Charlie the tide is out. Maybe we'll go out after we get the groceries home and stored. You need a good run having sat in the garage most of the winter. It was nice of Al and Penny to take you to Brown's Auto for a lube and oil change last week. I need a good run too. I've got to get this weight off me so Dana and I can race to the north cliffs again. We did love that when we were kids. How lucky we are our end of the beach was selected to become the State Park. Busy as it is it still has some wildness that was here when we were kids. The red cliffs and the smooth boulder at its base are our touchstones and we'd race to be the first to pound that round stone stuck in the cliff face and shout, 'I declare this run good and done.'"

Suddenly Eliza begins to cry. Turning the Jeep onto the shoulder of the road she grabs some tissue from a box under the dash and wipes her eyes. "What the hell is this all about? These memories are coming too fast. It's as if my Dad's riding with us right now. Of course he isn't. He died in that accident when I was ten. When I married Jack, Mom remarried and moved to Portland. I'm so excited about finally being at Redcliff's and these feelings are overwhelming. Also I just realized I haven't eaten anything today. We'd better go get the groceries and get home to fix me some breakfast. Right, Charlie?"

As she nears the turnoff to Ocean Shores she notices the Jeep's gas gage is near the empty mark so she turns into the service station at the cutoff. While the attendant fills the tank she thinks again of Jack and the reasons she stayed with him so many years. "We had no children. Why would I stay married to him? For darling Minna of course who agreed to give me all the voting shares in the company along with total ownership of the Staples Mansion if I stayed and watched over Jack after she died. Those shares were worth a million then and millions now. After I took over the helm I built the company into the international giant it is now and earned every penny."

Eliza closes her eyes and remembers. *We were best friends Minna and I. I was more to her than either Jack or her asshole husband. Mel the bastard should have been shot for the way he treated her and long before he taught Jack every obscene trick he knew. Good thing Mel died before Minna. She inherited all his shares in the company and the Staples Mansion and she passed them on to me. When her will was read Jack was furious and threatened to kill me right there in the lawyers' office. I was so frightened. I stayed in their offices until my new will was written. The new will gave Jack a salary of two hundred thousand plus yearly bonuses and his rooms at the Mansion as long as I live.*

I don't know what he does with his money but he whines continuously about how broke he is. He should be able live a damn good life on that sort of play money. He certainly doesn't do anything to earn it and doesn't spend it on anything obvious. How surprised he was when I divorced him years ago. Almost as surprised as when I told him I was moving to the beach house once the house was remodeled. His face lit up so I reminded him he only lives at the Mansion as long as I'm alive. When I die it will be turned over to the county's school system with a trust to fund its use and upkeep.

A tapping on the window wakens Eliza from her daydream and she quickly hands the station attendant her credit card then signs the slip when he brings it to her. At that time she notices her hands are shaking badly and her heart is pounding. She must get something to eat.

Before she can start the Jeep though a pickup drives up beside the Jeep and a man inside calls down to her, "How's the house fitting you Mrs. Staples?" Recognizing the man as the contractor who did the remodeling Eliza responds. "It's wonderful Stan and please it's Eliza. You must stop by if you're up that way to see your good work now that it's being lived in. Thanks for doing such a great job." As she waits for him to drive away she realizes she feels very lightheaded.

Turning the Jeep towards the small drive-in across from the service station she orders a milkshake. When the shake arrives she gulps it down hoping it will calm the shaking of her hands. When it doesn't, she grips the steering wheel to hold them still. "Why am I feeling like this? I'm at the beach. I love the beach. All I needed was a bit of food. I haven't felt this way since before I was diagnosed bipolar manic depressive and I haven't been this far down since my meds balanced me out. Not since my meds? Oh no, my God my meds. I didn't take my meds. Why? I always do before I shower. Where did I put them? Did I take them last night? Oh no, it was before I left the Mansion for Staples yesterday morning. The medicine bag is by the kitchen sink. Two sets of pills. I've missed two sets of pills. Charlie we've got to go to the Mansion and get my meds."

Without much thought Eliza turns the Jeep onto SH109 and drives through the small towns along the way without really seeing them. Within the hour she is on I-205 South heading towards the Columbia River Bridge near Portland. Her mind races in all directions until it lands upon the day she first met Jack. "It had to be love; I wouldn't have settled for less at that time. It was love for us both for those first ten years. He loved me before that damn Mel decided I was too soft and demanded Jack teach me to handle guns so I could hunt with the two of them."

Her head rings so loudly Eliza feels as if she wants to vomit, "Oh God I'm so sick and its miles to the Mansion. Breathe deep and calm down Eliza. Drive carefully. Take the meds by noon. Have a peanut butter and jelly sandwich. You'll be okay, OK? Where was I? Yeah those damn guns Mel kept pushing at me till I knew how to load and clean every damn one of them blindfolded. I did it for Jack and for the peace and quiet Minna got when I was Mel's target.

"I loaded shot and cleaned every damn one of those guns for her and Jack. Even then Jack loved me until Mel took him to South America on those fruit sales trips twenty years ago. He came back a different man. Said he'd seen how real men live so he knew what a wife should do for their man. Jack came back a bastard just like Mel. Minna saw it too and it broke her heart more than it did mine. Darling Minna she would have killed Mel if he hadn't died of a heart attack soon after."

The miles fly past as Eliza pushes the Jeep to its maximum speed. When she finally crosses the Columbia River Bridge she knows she is getting close to home. During the miles on I-80 East it feels as if someone else is driving the Jeep and she is surprised when the exit onto the road up to the Mansion is suddenly there. The Jeep turns onto it then crosses back over the freeway and drives up the hill to a pair of forbidding iron gates. Eliza automatically keys the numbers into the keypad and the gates swing open allowing the Jeep to enter. Exhausted by the drive and the lack of medications she drives on without looking back knowing the gates will close on their own. Soon she turns into a narrow lane which weaves around a thick grove of evergreens ending at the back of the large Victorian Mansion she had called home for thirty years.

Eliza parks the Jeep close to the kitchen door at the back of the house. After she unlocks the back door and steps inside she automatically taps in the code numbers to turn off the security alarm. Walking into the kitchen she sees her medicine bag on the counter and immediately shakes out the needed pills from the bottles. As soon as she fills a glass with water she swallows the meds and sighs with relief. Leaning against the counter for a long moment Eliza shivers as she calculates how close she had come to losing herself.

"My God it's almost noon. That was way too close for comfort and way too stupid for words. Now I'll have to sleep until late afternoon. Well there's no hurry now. I'll have a late dinner in Portland." Knowing the side effects of the pills will make it impossible to drive safely for a few hours before she adjusts to them Eliza takes the medicine bag out to the Jeep, tucks it under the seat next to her purse then sticks the key into the ignition and walks back into the house. When she comes inside she makes and eats a thick peanut butter and jelly sandwich and drinks a large glass of milk. Afterward she carefully puts the glass, knife, and plate into the dishwasher then wipes off the counter with a paper towel which she tosses into the garbage under the sink.

Already feeling the effects of the pills she walks through the massive house to the large circular foyer with high solid entry doors with stained glass panels on each side. Across from the grand entry is a set of equally impressive French doors which open into a large room that spreads along the back of the mansion. Minna called this room the library as it is filled with leather furniture, hardwood floors covered with Turkish rugs and walls paneled in dark woods with built in shelves showing the Staples' family history amongst leather-bound first editions, family photos, awards and artifacts stuffed everywhere. Along the room's back wall is a ceiling high native stone fireplace surrounded by magnificent glassed and locked display cases which hold Grandfather Staples' impressive collection of antique pistols, rifles, and holsters each with boxes of ammunition. These are the very guns Eliza learned to shoot and clean.

Studying them through the window cases, the last gun she handled seems to loom at Eliza and she stares at it for several seconds. "Oh yes my friend there you are the rarest of antiques. Thank God I dropped you that final day. Mel called me a clumsy damned bitch and told me to get out of his sight. I told him to go burn in hell I was done being his whipping post." Eliza laughs loudly enjoying the thought of Mel Staples sitting amongst flames.

"Being in this room brings back too many memories. No wonder I avoided it after Minna died." Eliza rubs her forehead and yawns. The pills and the long drive are quickly taking their toll so she pulls two wool throws off the back of the long leather sofas and covers the seat of one sofa with one of the throws. Tucking a small pillow in one end she pulls the second throw over her legs as she lies down and is asleep as soon as her head touches the pillow.

Just before two in the afternoon Eliza is startled awake by a loud blast of noise. Jumping to her feet her heart pounds and she looks wildly around the room completely puzzled as to where she is. Her head spins so much she falls back onto the sofa. Sitting for some while before her eyes finally focus she studies the high stone fireplace until she remembers how she happens to be at the Staples Mansion. Looking at her watch she snorts, "Don't know what woke me but it's only two p.m. I need more sleep before I head back to the beach."

Then remembering the noise she decides to check the house and goes to the open French door. From where she stands she can see the entry doors in the foyer are shut. "Hello? Is anybody there?" she calls out. As if in answer a horn blasts and is followed by a screech of laughter and a man's voice yelling, "I'm so horny I'm honking," followed by more screeching laughter.

Familiar emotions rush through Eliza disgust, betrayal, anger felt every time Jack fell in lust with another woman. A good dozen or more by her count of the ones she knew or suspected and the ones who rejected him told her they'd done so. Good friends or so-called friends made certain to tell her about all of them. Walking through the entry she looks out the side panel and sees Jack's large Mercedes parked at the wide sweep of steps to the front door. The car is bouncing and rocking back and forth. Inside she sees a couple grappling on the front seat. Clothes are tossed out the driver's window. It's Jack with one of his bitches.

Eliza whirls away and runs through the house and past the kitchen into the maid's bathroom. She collapses beside the open toilet and vomits into the bowl. Residues of medications and peanut butter and jelly sandwich float on the water and she spits into it shaking and nauseous. When finished she pulls a large wad of toilet paper off the roll and wipes her mouth. Standing at the sink she turns the cold water tap on and splashes water over her face and rinses her mouth. Drying her face and hands with a towel hanging next to the sink she then wipes the sink and toilet with the same and buries the towel in the basket of dirty laundry. Finally she flushes the toilet and shuts the lid. Still feeling faint she sits on the toilet lid with her head in her hands trying to think of what her next action should be.

She moans, "What more do I have to take. What more can he do to me? Thank God we never had children neither for Minna nor for me. What a horrid father he'd have been. Almost thirty years with that bastard and his fucking around. Never again will I hear snickers or be the butt of every foul joke in town. He will never do this to me again!"

In that instant she remembers the guns. Turning she hurries into the kitchen and opens the cabinet under the sink. Picking up a box of rubber gloves she pulls a pair from it and slips them onto her hands. Then she drops the box back where it had been and closes the cabinet door before walking back to the den. Standing just inside the library's open French door she still sees movement in the car. Closing the French door she walks to the cabinet that holds the gun of her choice Grandfather Staples' old pistol, the one she had dropped.

Reaching along one side of the cabinet she presses a spot under the molding strip at the far corner. There is a click just before the glass doors slowly swing open. Reaching inside she lifts the heavy pistol off the elegant silver display rack. Beside it sits a small box of ammunition. "Grandfather Staples your old-west six-shooter is going to kill a dirty rat." She nods as a smile twists her mouth. "It's a good thing to use. After all the rats, rabid dogs, and dirty bastards you killed with it my doing in one more dirty rotten bastard won't matter."

As if it had been yesterday she remembers the routine Mel Staples had demanded and Eliza opens the gun's barrel takes six bullets from the ammo box and slips one into each of the six chambers then snaps the gun closed. Walking to the room's

French doors she pulls one wide open so she can fully see the foyer. Then she turns the nearest wing-backed chair to face the door before she sits in it to wait.

Suddenly Eliza sees movement on the porch through the entry's side window and raises the gun. Then she lowers it to her lap as the front door slams open with a loud thud followed by a naked couple rushing to the sweeping staircase. It is Jack with a woman Eliza can't see clearly enough to recognize. He holds the woman's buttocks as he grinds his pelvis against her on every step up the stairs. A small suitcase sits ignored in the doorway. Eliza freezes as the couple moves up the stairwell. Hate and anger rage through her in sweeping waves of emotion. She doesn't move, can't move though the couple disappears at the top of the stairs their gross sounds come down to her as shrieks of laughter and cursing. Suddenly it's quiet for several minutes then water can be heard running somewhere above her. Then as if an ugly naked puppet Jack is leaping down the stairs yelling, "Get your ass in that tub woman! I'll get the drinks."

The woman screams with laughter then yells, "Forget the wine Jack. Get that big cock back in here."

More laughter and obscene words ring through the house. Eliza raises the gun off her lap as Jack races past the open door. Shortly there is banging of cabinet doors and slamming of drawers in the kitchen then he hurries back past the door holding a bottle and two fluted glasses over his head shouting, "Ready or not here I come!"

Only then does Eliza move. Slowly she walks to the French door to watch Jack's nakedness bounce up the stairs. As she walks into the entry she stops to look at the pieces of clothing left on the stoop. Pushing the small suitcase in the doorway with her toe she frowns with disgust. Then she turns and follows Jack up the stairs. It's as if she is watching another person move.

ELIZA

I must be invisible. Jack passed the open door twice without seeing me. The thought brings a bubble of laughter into her throat that stays there as she reaches the top landing and turns down the hall to Jack's room where she silently opens the door. As she steps inside the room she raises the gun and her finger tightens on the trigger. Then she stops and stares. There is no one inside the room or on the bed. Stunned she tries to think where they could be. Then a shriek comes from the opposite end of the hall and her breath leaves her as if someone has punched her in the stomach. Her heart pounds causing her head to throb. "That bastard he's taken his slut to my room and is rutting on my bed."

Rage propels her down the hall to the open door of what had been her room for thirty years. She hears Jack groan. Then she hears the woman smack her lips as Jack's groans come louder and faster. Stepping into the room Eliza goes to the foot of the bed. It looks as if there is one strangely shaped person moving amongst a pile of bedding. Within the odd shape she sees the bare buttocks of a woman. Her head is in Jack's crotch. Eliza sees him thrust his pelvis at the woman's face and sees his hand pull at thick blond hair as his orgasm comes.

That is when Eliza again points the gun. This time she pulls the trigger shooting the woman directly through the back of her head into Jack's groin. Then she shoots Jack in the chest and again in the middle of his forehead, contract killer style clean and neat. For several seconds Eliza stares at the couple watching for signs of life. Seeing no movement she tips the gun upward and blows the smoke from the barrel end. "The only good rat is a dead rat." She grins and the hysterical bubble of laughter she held back bursts from her throat as a sob.

Then her thoughts come quickly as if a checklist. *Turn air conditioner to forty degrees to keep the bodies cold. Time of death will be hard to determine as they'll keep cold for days. No fingerprints left as have on rubber gloves. Now shut door and go down stairs.* Eliza carefully follows each of her instructions and when she is again at the entry door she looks out at Jack's car parked close to the front stoop. The driver's door is open. For a moment she considers moving it to the garage and shutting the entry doors. Then seeing the clothes and suitcase she snorts with disgust and walks back to the library.

From a drawer within the display case she takes out a gun-cleaning kit. Then she carefully pulls apart the pistol cleaning every part even the empty shells and unused bullets. She wipes each carefully with the rag from the kit before returning them to the ammunition box. Then she returns the pistol to its display rack and places the ammo box where it had been. Carefully folding and replacing the cleaning cloth as it had been she puts the cleaning kit back into the drawer closes it and pushes the glass door closed until she hears the firm click of the lock.

Walking to where she had napped she folds the two woolen throws and returns them to where she'd found them. Then she pats the small pillow back into its spot and turns the wing-backed chair back to face the fireplace. As she scans the room for signs she'd been there she peels off the rubber gloves tucking one inside the other until they form a tight ball. Then with a great sense of relief and no sense of loss Eliza closes the French door then walks through the kitchen and goes out the back door shutting it behind her. As she steps into the driver's seat of the Jeep she says, "OK Charlie, take me home. It's been a long day."

Just as she turns onto I-80 West it begins to rain. "Good. Rain will wash away your tire marks." Eliza tells the Jeep. By the time she reaches the bridge over the Columbia River the rain has turned into a downpour. Halfway across the expanse Eliza slows the Jeep and moves as close to the right side of the bridge as she safely can. Seeing no traffic close behind her she opens the window on her side and heaves the balled gloves over the top of the Jeep and bridge railing to the river below.

CHAPTER FOUR

JUNE 10th

LIZ

LIZ lost the days following Peter's death. Nothing mattered anymore since the one person she valued above her own life was gone. Peter's death left a vast void into which she has fallen. She manages to move through each day thanking visitors for whatever they offer without feeling or notice. Alex comes to her door daily with offers to help sort through Peter's things. Each time Liz sends her away with a shake of her head and a wave of her hand closing the door on her neighbor and friend. Trying to avoid Alex's advances as well as other well-meaning people who come to aid her Liz finds her solace at the edge of the waves trekking north to the red-rocked cliffs before dawn and again late at night.

When Peter's ashes arrive by Federal Express late on the afternoon of the tenth of June she is forced back into the present reality of her life. Holding the neatly wrapped package the driver hands to her Liz is surprised by small size of the package. She carries it to the kitchen counter and takes a pair of scissors to carefully open it. Inside is a sturdy black box with Peter's name on top along with the words "CREMATION NUMBER 2200991." Lifting the lid off the box she finds inside a plastic sack filled with ashes. Pulling the sack out of the box she holds it in both hands amazed at how truly little is left of a six-foot-five-inch man weighing almost two hundred pounds.

She studies the sack for several minutes trying to get her mind around her next step. Looking out the front slider doors she sees the tide is ebbing and this makes her decision easy. Putting the sack of ashes back into the box and the box into a small backpack Liz leaves her house and heads up the beach to the cliffs. As she goes she focuses on her duty to Peter telling him why she must lay him on this outgoing tide. "I can't keep you on the mantle for even one day my darling as you told me all these years you'd haunt me if I did that. So my love, it's off to the red cliffs and today's ebbing tide."

At the base of the cliffs Liz climbs onto the smooth red boulder slaps the round stone embedded in the vertical cliff and shouts, "I declare this run good and done!" The few people near the cliffs are too absorbed in their own day to give her much notice as she swings the backpack off her shoulders and sets it on the boulder. Then she lifts the box lid and pulls out the sack of ashes. As she does a rush of feelings flow through her and she presses the sack to her heart.

Then she quickly slits the sack's top edge with her penknife and holds Peter's ashes into both arms. Stepping off the boulder Liz splashes through tidal pools until she is past the cliff's point to where the waves are still sucking outward. Once she feels this pull of the tide on her feet and legs she stops. Holding the sack she empties the ashes onto the outgoing waves. "Go with God my love. You are done with this life. Fly free and soar through the universe. I love you and always will. I release you on these waves at this place we both have loved for so long and so deeply."

The ash quickly swirls away on the ebbing tide and as she shakes out the last bits from the sack the dust is caught by the breeze and taken up along the cliff face. Liz watches until there is nothing to see. Then she wades back to the slab rock and stuffs the empty sack into the box and puts the box into the pack which she then slings over her shoulders. Climbing onto the rock she again faces the cliff face and slaps the protruding red stone. "I declare this run truly good and done!"

Tears don't come until she is back in her home and curled up in Peter's chair with his woolen throw wrapped around her. It is then that Liz's sobs begin and continue until she sleeps. Hours later she awakens to see it is night and a soft rain spatters the windows. As she looks around the darkened room she is startled to see a soft glow coming from the ceiling down to light the center of the dining table.

Puzzled she walks to the table and looks up. The glow seems to come through a spot in the ceiling. While she watches the light intensifies into a broad beam that covers the table top. Rushing back to Peter's chair she pulls the throw over herself as if for protection. Slowly the beam of light shows three shadowy forms within it. To her surprise neither the beam of light nor the forms frighten her. Instead the vision comforts her and for the first time since Peter's death a peaceful calm comes over her. As she watches the images move within the light she feels Peter near her.

The fluctuating light becomes hypnotic and soon Liz falls into a deep sleep. When she awakens it is late the next morning and she is still wrapped in the throw on Peter's chair. Looking at the dining table where the beam of light had danced Liz smiles and knows without a doubt that the beam of light will return that coming night.

THE ELIZABETHS

Leaving the throw where it lays she fixes coffee and her first good meal since Peter's death. After that she begins to box up Peter's clothes. When that is done she hauls them out to her car and drives down to Ocean Shores to leave them at the Salvation Army store. She stops at the grocery to buy a large steak which she takes home and grills for dinner. The sunset is glorious. As Liz watches the colors sweep across the horizon she enjoys every bite of the rare beef along with two full glasses of a great Merlot Peter brought back from Tuscany. When sun has set and the last colors are leaving the sky Liz wraps herself in the warm throw and settles amongst the pile of pillows on the leather sofa to wait for the light to return.

When the beam of light does appear it is so intense it brightens the entire room. Startled Liz looks up from her book squinting against the glare and shouts, "Peter the light is too bright." At that time the glare dims and she again feels Peter's presence near her. Slowly the light softens to a golden glow letting the three shapes show clearly. Liz sees that Peter is facing her and he appears as the tall strong youth she fell in love with over thirty years before.

Behind him to his right stands a beautiful dark skinned woman and to his left is a tall dark man who looks very angry. As she watches these images the clothing on all three forms changes to gowns of white silk. At that time Liz can see each of the two forms faces a different woman in separate rooms beyond hers and that neither of these women responds to the visions facing them.

Liz watches the images within the beam of light for several minutes when Peter's voice comes through to her bringing a complete sense of loving peace which flows through her. With each word his image becomes clearer and soon she can see his lips move as his words fill her mind. He speaks faster and faster until he pulls her thoughts through every second, minute, day, week, and year of their life together. When these visions finish Liz realizes the intense grief she'd felt since losing Peter is gone. The black void left by his death is replaced with a joyous knowledge and strength for her future. As his words continue they embrace her in soft rhythms each word becoming a caress.

Live your own life Elizabeth. Love that life fully. Love all ways. Love always. Let no one turn you away from your truth. Rejoice in each day. Be thankful for each moment. Embrace what you have and are given. Time is naught. Know we exist all ways at all times. We choose each existence to experience that chosen. The choices are ours. We choose each that comes to us so love each for the experience it brings you. These teachers are how we grow within and through each life. Greet each new encounter as it comes to you. Learn these lessons brought for your life growth negative or positive. Apply all experience of all positive encounters to your future. Avoid negative beings. Understand that their beliefs lead circular life paths to be repeated again and again until that life lesson is learned. Remember love is all so fear no one. Accept yourself and your own actions. There is a reason for everything for there are no mistakes. You are a goddess. Love all who come to you. Do so with wisdom and joy.

The beam of light changes to deep gold as Peter's words change to warnings. Liz suddenly understands she must follow his demands. "Slow down Peter. I can't understand what it is that you want me to do. OK. Yes. All right darling I'll do that. I'll call Alex. What should I tell her? Come at once?" Without hesitation Liz picks up her cell phone from the end table next to the sofa and dials Alex's number. When her neighbor answers Liz says, "Alex, Liz. Please come over here right now. I need you to see something. Peter has come back and wants to speak to you. Please come right now this minute. I want you to see for yourself that he is here with me at this moment." Then she hangs up without giving Alexandria time to respond.

In the house north of Liz's Alexandria Petrow is stunned at what she's heard. Puzzled she shouts into the dead phone,

"Liz? What do you mean? You want me now? I mean…Liz? Vat you say? Liz? Vat you say?" Then she stares at the phone realizing Liz has hung up. Grabbing a windbreaker and flashlight Alex hurries down the steps of her deck to the path through the woods leading to Liz's home and sees the house is totally dark as she climbs the steps to the deck. Alex runs to the glass slider. Looking into the dark room as she slides the door open she shouts, "Liz where you? Liz? Vat you said? Liz? Vat you say? Damn it Liz. Where are you?"

"Here on the sofa Alex. Come sit by me. Look there on the dining table. See the beam of light in the center of it? Peter is in that beam of light. He's come to tell me what I need to know for my future. He took me on a wonderful journey through our lifetime together. Now he wants to talk with you. Come over here to the sofa and sit by me."

Pointing the flashlight in the direction of Liz's voice Alex sees her on the sofa and asks, "Liz? It's Alex. Are you okay, Liz?"

Smiling Liz looks at her friend. "Yes Alex. I'm more than okay. Look over there. See the beam of light coming through the ceiling and lighting up the top of the table? Peter's in it with two other people. He says not to worry about them as I'll know more about them later. Right now he needs to talk to you about something. So sit and be quiet. He'll tell you what he wants you to know."

Stunned Alex gasps and stares at Liz in disbelief. "What did you say? Liz? Have you gone nuts? Why would you say that?"

Liz laughs as she points at the table. "Alex you must see him. Peter is right in front of us in that beam of light. Don't you see the light on the dining table?"

Alex shakes her head. "No I don't," she shouts as she runs to the table and slaps her hands across the top of it. "No Liz!

LIZ

There is nothing on this table. Not Peter. Not a beam of light with other people in it. There is nothing!"

Liz cries out and rushes over to Alexandria and pulls the woman back to the sofa. "Don't do that. Come here and sit still. All you've done is make the light disappear for a while. Now we'll have to wait until it comes back with Peter and the others in it. Don't worry though he always comes back. And he insists he needs to talk to you. Sit here beside me and wait. He says he has an important message just for you."

Alex sits stiffly on the edge of the sofa and stares at Liz as if seeing her for the first time. "My God Liz you've gone crazy."

Laughing Liz says, "No Alex I'm not crazy. You'll see for yourself soon enough. Peter will come back and talk to you. See? There's the beam of light now and Peter's in it. Do you see him? He's in the middle of the beam. I told you he always comes back. At first the light was so bright I couldn't tell what it was that I saw. At that time I only heard Peter's words. Only when the light softened could I see him clearly. Of course I know it's not really Peter but his essence, soul or whatever you want to call it. And he'll leave forever once he's told me what I need to know."

"Liz you must not imagine such things. Peter is dead. You must know that if you don't stop this you'll go mad."

"Of course he's dead Alex. I realize that. Peter was cremated. I spread his ashes on the outgoing tide at the base of the cliff two days ago. There Alex don't you see? Peter's in the beam of light on the table and wants to talk to you. Don't you see the light? It's so beautiful and Peter's in the middle. What Peter? OK? Yes I'll tell her. Peter wants you to sit close to me and he will talk to you through me and only you will hear him or know what he tells you."

"What did you say?" Alex demands. "Why would you say that to me? I have nothing to say to Peter's ghost. What are you trying to do Liz? Why are you doing this to me? Damn it to hell I'm telling you that Peter is not here!"

Stunned by the harshness of Alex's words Liz shouts at her, "Yes Alex he is here and he says for you to sit down by me and listen. He says he knows many things about you and those around you. You are no clairvoyant. No. So sit down and shut-up. Listen to what he has to say. Be quiet. He says to tell you that you are in great danger so listen to him if you want to live."

Liz turns her attention to the table. "Yes Peter she knows where to look. No she doesn't see the light. Can't you talk to her in her mind as you did to me? OK, I'll do that.

"Alex Peter says I'm to be quiet so you can hear him speak through me. I am going to sleep for a while so he can speak. Stay right here beside me." With that Liz leans back against the sofa and closes her eyes.

Alex watches Liz close her eyes and take several deep breaths. Then she hears a voice that would be Peter's if he was in the room with her yet it is coming from Liz's mouth. "Alex you are not who you say you are yet exactly who you truly are. You are both known and unknown. You hide at Redcliff's as Liz's friend yet you travel far as our enemy. You are to be held accountable by those who have felt your sting. Your presence is known. The Universal judgment waits to review your life when you arrive. Your truth is known Alex. Know this. We exist within the one omnipresent omnipotent universal energy which is all there is and ever will be. Everything is known all ways at all times. Understand this. Know it. Your life has been evaluated as your choices have been clear. You will die soon. Know the time and place are your choice. Remember what I say. The choice is yours alone."

Alex's eyes widen as she stares at the table in the center of the room and begins to see a soft golden glow of light emanate from the ceiling. The beam brightens and soon covers the top of the dining table. She sees Peter's image within it. He faces her. Behind him stand a black woman and a dark haired man facing other directions.

Alex gasps for air and shivers violently. "Liz I see him. Peter's there just as you said. Others are with him. Damn the light's so bright I need to squint. I mean too bright light…oh crap why bother he knew everything all the time." Gasping for breath Alex speaks without her accent and turns to see it Liz has noticed. Though Liz still sleeps Alex shakes her awake. Holding onto one of Liz's hands Alex shouts, "Liz? You come back? You hear Peter's words? Words he said to me?"

Rubbing her eyes Liz shakes her head, "No Alex I didn't hear what he said to you. I guess I fell asleep. So you did see him. I can tell you did, didn't you? What's that Peter? He says for you to go home. Choose your future wisely. Now he wants me to meet my others. I don't know what that means. Is that what you called them Peter my others? What are they? I mean who are they? Peter? Yes. Okay, I'll listen. Sorry Alex. Peter says you must go and you must remember his words. Make the right choice and you live. The choice is yours, live or die. My goodness Peter those are rather harsh words aren't they?"

"You heard what Peter said to me? Liz?"

"Of course I did this time as he spoke to me so I can tell you. Not before though when I fell asleep and he spoke directly to you through me. I was asleep that time. I told you Alex. Just now though he told me to tell you to go home and to choose to live or die. I wonder why he would say that. Do you know Alex? Alex? You did see Peter didn't you Alex? Didn't you? Ouch. Alex you're twisting my arm. Stop it Alex. You're hurting me!"

"Yes Liz I saw your damned Peter." Alexandria Petrow shouts as she drops Liz's hand and stands. "Yes damn you fool I saw that dead husband of yours in that beam of light with two others behind him. Yes damn it I saw him. Now I tell you to tell him to go to hell. Damn Peter. Damn you Liz." Then without another word Alex grabs her flashlight off the dining table and rushes out the slider door and vanishes into the rainy night.

For several seconds Liz stares at the open slider then as the rain beats its way inside she hurries over to close and lock it against the stormy night. When she returns to the sofa she hears Peter's voice. *Do not speak to Alexandria of her not having her accent. Not one word. You heard correctly. She spoke without an accent. Say nothing. Alex is dangerous. She can no longer hide in Redcliff's therefore you must give her space and time to flee. Know she is your enemy. Now you must meet your others.*

Liz frowns. "My others Peter you keep saying that. What do you mean my others? Aren't the man and woman with you those others?"

No the two with me are known only by your others. They existed together in past lifetimes as we did in ours. Your others are who each of the two face. Your others will come to you and you will soon know them. You are of one entity though your lives split from each other and you each lived different lives in separate dimensions. Each will come to you. Watch for them. Speak softly while questioning. Eventually they will see you also. As the summer solstice nears you will know each other. They will come to you in your home for you each have lived within this common place of your father's cabin before and after you became parallel lives of the other.

As Peter finishes speaking his image fades from within the beam of light and the two behind him become clearer. The man in the beam of light looks very angry as Liz watches him. He waves his arms and seems to be shouting at a woman tucked into the corner of a long white leather sectional sofa in a room that spreads far beyond Liz's dining table. The furniture in this room is modern with white tiled floors and a white marble fireplace. The sofa length extends across a commanding view of the ocean through a series of high French doors. Tonight the woman is reading a book and every so often she reaches to her left to pick up a tall crystal wine glass off a long ebony table behind the sofa. After taking a sip of the wine she sets the stemware on the table and returns to her book. This woman looks well tended or what Peter used to call a person of high maintenance. Her hair is shoulder length and white. To Liz the woman belongs within the lush modern surroundings.

The man in the beam of light seems to scream his wrath at this woman and pounds his fists together whenever the woman turns to pick up the wine glass. His mouth opens wide with his silent screams. As this woman continues not to notice him the man becomes frantic and rips the silk clothing from his body. Then his actions become wilder the woman turns to look over the back of the sofa as if reacting to his tantrums. Instead she picks a remote off the table aims it across the room and instantly Liz hears soft jazz dance across through the room. When the woman does this she looks directly at Liz for several seconds.

Gasping with recognition Liz sees herself in the woman. Though she has longer hair and is heavier the woman has Liz's eyes, nose, chin, cheekbones and mouth. Each of those features could be Liz's own. "I don't understand. Peter who is she? Why does that man hate her so much? Why did you bring them to me at this time?" Liz wants answers. Instead she hears only one word: *Watch.*

Then the beam of light changes as the image of the man dims and the willowy young black woman comes through. This woman is beautiful in all ways. She is leaning forward as if to step into the room beyond. This room is very different than the other. It is a small room with only a few antique pieces mixed around an old brown leather sofa and chair along the room's north wall which is in the middle of Liz's own room. A wooden table sits directly in the middle of the room and meshes along one side with her dining table. These tables are where the beam of light is showing Liz the three images. Four wooden chairs sit around this table. Rain is beating on a set of glass slider doors out to a deck.

Liz gasps with delight. "Peter it's my old cabin. It's my folks' cabin! It's just as before we remodeled it. Even the sliders are the same. Holy cow Peter it fits within our own home. I hadn't realized how much we added onto all sides. Peter look at that woman who sits on the old sofa! She's me in every way. Even has the hair I had before I got my summer cut."

Liz studies the woman's hair held up in a ponytail tied by a scarf. Then she looks at the other on the white leather sofa. Both women fit their own spaces and Liz realizes she herself fits comfortably within her own home. "Peter I see that they are of me. They must be. Yet how can we exist within this same space and not know each other? That modern room is huge and extends way past my walls in all directions while the cabin fits within my own home. Where do they exist if I'm here and they are also? Why don't we know each other?"

As Liz watches, the woman on the white leather sofa continues to read never noticing the angry man in the shaft of light. Amazed at both the amount of anger from the man and the indifference of the woman Liz feels a bit frightened. With this emotion Peter's voice fills her mind again. *Do not fear. He can no longer hurt her. Though she caused his death his negative energy is repulsed by her opposing greater energy. His anger turns back to him as lightning striking a long-dead tree. Each repulse of anger is sent back to him twice as powerful twice as meaningful. See him cringe. Yet he doesn't cease his hatred. The omnipresent omnipotent universal energy will intervene to level and humble him. His negatives are so many and so strong they are erasing her negative karma which comes from her one passionate action of taking two lives during her long positive lifetime.*

To Liz it's as if she's watching a film and she half believes what she sees while the other half denies what she is seeing. Suddenly there are several loud cracking flashes which stun the man in the light beam and he drops to his knees looking upward. As the light around him darkens to a red glow the man covers his head with his arms. A light flashes bright white blinding Liz for several seconds. When she can again see only Peter and the black woman are in the light beam. The angry man is gone.

Liz gasps. "Peter what happened to that man?"

The negative karma of his past life sent him to return to live a life treated by another as he has done in this life. He must learn the lesson of unconditional love without setting conditions or having anger. If he can not he will return after each death to live a harsher life until he lives a truly humble life loving it as he lives it. See the woman respond to his leaving. See that she now softens the music as his negative force is no longer distorting her positive energy.

"Peter I see both of the others beyond the beam of light. Are they of me or am I of them? Which Peter?

Instead of an answer the beam of golden light disappears from the room. At the same moment the floors and ceilings of the three homes flow together meshing within the center of the rooms where her dining table touches the other two dining tables. Excited Liz goes to her own table and calls out, "Hello over there can anybody hear me? I'm Liz Day. Who are you?" When neither woman reacts she calls out again, "Hello there? Do you see me? Can you see each other? Which of you ran beside me on the beach the day that Peter died?"

Suddenly a wind gust slams against the north side of the house rattling a lose shutter as sleet pellets beat on the windows and in response Liz hurries through the house checking for open windows. When she returns the beam of light and the women in their rooms are gone. Though at first she is disappointed she finds after a few minutes she doesn't mind. Peter has left her with much to think over and Liz feels as if she has seen all she can absorb for one night. "Thank you for coming back to me my love. I will never forget you. I was not ready to lose you. I would never have been ready to lose you. Damn that plane crash."

At the mention of the plane crash Peter's voice fills her head once more. *The crash was caused by another. Demand Bob investigate. I leave you now. Mourn no more. Release me for I must go elsewhere. Your others will meet you soon. Remember to avoid Alex. Know my love for you is eternal. All love is eternal.*

Early the next morning Liz calls Bob Drake. A phone message tells her he is out of the office so she leaves the message that he should investigate the plane crash. When she hangs up the phone she pours a mug of coffee and goes to sit at her dining table. Instantly she sees the other rooms have again joined with hers and the two women are each standing near the doors to their own decks.

"Hello there. I'm so glad you're both here with me. I'm Elizabeth Ann Anderson. Is that also your names? Can you hear me or see me? Please try to so we can get to know each other," Liz says softly.

The woman in the cabin looks at Liz then shouts, "Who are you?" Then she turns bumping into the woman by the French doors. She looks at the woman there and shouts at her, "You're the woman who ran through my house before Maxine died. How did you get in here?"

LIZ

Though this woman shows no indication that she hears or sees either of the women Liz answers for them all. "We're each Elizabeth Ann Andersons. I'm Liz Day. We share a connection where our homes are. Can you come to the tables and talk with me. We seem to be part of a very unusual paradox."

"Who said that? Who's there?" The woman at the French doors moves toward the ebony dining table where it attaches to both Liz's and the one in the cabin. Liz stands to greet her. "I spoke. I'm Elizabeth Anderson Day. Who are you?" As Liz talks the woman walks toward Liz holding one hand out to her until their hands touch. Instantly both women disappear and Liz is alone in her own home.

CHAPTER FIVE

JUNE 10th

BETH

BETH watches Dana's car back wildly up the driveway. When the car reaches the road it turns and speeds south on Shoreline Drive. "And don't come back!" Beth shouts shaking her fist at the vanishing car. "That sister of mine needs some anger management classes. What a truly horrible bitch she is. No wonder her daughters are fleeing from her as soon as they can and Ed is divorcing her. Please dear God let this be the last time I ever have to explain to that bitch that the beach cabin is no longer mine. It belongs to the State of Washington. I only get to stay here until I die or it is washed out to sea."

As she turns back to the cabin a gust of wind picks the lids off the three garbage cans she left in the back of her pickup and sends them sailing up the drive. When they land each rolls a different direction. Beth races to catch them and returns them to the cans. "Thank goodness I emptied these cans this morning. I'd be chasing trash for seven miles," she grumbles to herself as she transfers the cans from the pickup to inside the carport and secures them to brass hooks her dad put there years before. Then she hurries down the side deck to drag the deck chairs and pads into the protective el of the carport.

"The last thing I need is for everything to get blown onto the beach. Those storm clouds look as if they're bringing in a big one. Maybe some rain will come with the wind for a change. Things are pretty dry." Suddenly she stops and laughs. "Oh good lord now I'm talking to myself. Max I miss you. I need something live around me something to talk to. Maybe I'd better get a pet before I get hauled to the loony bin."

However as Beth secures the deck furniture in the carport she is still talking to herself. "Stop feeling sorry for yourself. Maxine fought the good fight as long as she could bear it." Finally the deck is cleared of everything except the round table which she ties to two deck supports. As she turns to go inside a hard gust of wind shakes the cabin bringing with it a pounding rain. Quickly closing the door behind her Beth watches the winds sweep high rollers across the flattened beach. Then as if it might help secure the cabin from the storm she bolts the door.

"Here comes another one Max. Today is not a good day. Dana came again this afternoon. I thought she was here to comfort me. But no all she wanted was to berate me for giving the land to the State. Dad was so wise. He always told me, 'Pick your friends with great care as you are born into a family and you're stuck with the nuts in it.' And I need to call the Sheriff and report that nut was here violating the injunction against her. Let's hope this is the last time I have to do it."

A lose shutter bangs against the north side of the cabin. Getting her small toolbox from under the sink Beth rushes out to tighten the hinge then closes and locks it and the other shutters over each window. Once this is done she walks the perimeter of the cabin to check for anything that might take flight with the wind.

The sky darkens by the minute as Beth returns to the cabin and she turns on the lamp by the sofa and one in the kitchen. Quickly making a tuna salad sandwich and pouring a glass of milk she takes it to the table to eat. Next to the plate is the book Maxine gave her last Christmas and Beth opens it to read while she eats. She is enjoying the book even though she knows Max would not have liked her reading it while eating when a soft voice behind her startles her. Beth marks her place in the book and turns to look around the room when the voice repeats, "Hello there do you hear me?"

Laughing Beth answers, "Yes I do. Where are you?"

Again the voice speaks, "Hello I'm Elizabeth Anderson Day. Who are you?"

Beth answers, "I'm Elizabeth Ann Anderson. Where are you Dana? I know that's you. What kind of tricks are you trying to pull? What are you doing here? Where are you?" The only sounds she hears are those of the incoming storm. Still Beth checks both bedrooms and the bathroom. Finding no one she walks back to the table and returns to the book.

A sudden glow of light covers the table in front of her and startles her. Beth drops the book and pushes out of her chair backing away to the sofa. Staring at the beam of light she sees movement within it and gasps, "My God I am going mad. I must be. What else can this be?" Circling the table she watches the beam with an odd mix of horror and delight. Then she suddenly shouts, "Maxine it's you! It is. Oh Max what are you doing here? Was it you who talked to me earlier? Was that you? Max?" Beth gasps at the vision in front of her and sinks onto the sofa.

Staring at the beautiful black woman in the beam of light Beth begins to cry with joy. "It is you darling you are here." This Maxine is young and more beautiful than when Beth first met her in the Graduate Library. Then they were both exhausted from long hard hours working toward PhDs. Only after both achieved their goals did they regain some of their youthful looks and Maxine became the elegant full-bodied woman Beth loved for thirty years. This Maxine is a younger version and stands within a shaft of bright light on the center of the table. Beth's heart pounds as she watches with disbelief. This image sways within the light smiling tenderly and reaches out to Beth. This young face is filled with compassion and longing and love.

Beth moves close to the table and she wants to shout with joy or scream or flee or fall onto her knees and cry. She does none of these. When she reaches the table she simply enjoys the wonder of being in the presence of Maxine. When the image holds out her hands Beth is unable to stop and reaches into the light taking hold of both hands. Instantly the image disappears.

Stunned Beth backs up to the sofa and sits. Tears flood her eyes. Then a sense of peaceful energy surrounds her as she stares at the tabletop. She does not move or speak and is almost afraid to breathe. Several minutes pass before the shaft of light returns to the table bringing Maxine with it. *Yes I am here with you my darling Beth. Feel my love, my gratitude. You were always there for me. You are the best there is. I feel your intense loss, your deep pain. Let them go. We knew only joy and love. Feel that again. You will join me when it is your time. Not sooner. Till then know my love continues. Love others who will come to you. They are near and will soon come through to you. There is also a youth who needs guidance. Be there for her. Be kind. She needs your love more than ever.*

Maxine's voice fills Beth's mind. Wiping her eyes with the back of her hand she snuffles loudly. "I can't help this Maxine. You know I always cry when I'm happy. Oh Max you are here! It's so wonderful so beautiful to see you again my darling my dearest, so wonderful." Again she reaches into the beam of light. Again it vanishes.

"Damn it. I'll stop doing that just come back to me. Please Max. I don't want to lose you. Not this night. Please come back," Beth pleads as she sits on the sofa waiting for the light to return with Maxine. After several minutes she gets up to walk to the slider door and looks out at the storm. "What if she never returns? Max please come back to me. I won't try to touch you again. I'll behave."

When she turns back to the room Maxine is again in the beam of light on the table. She smiles as Beth walks to the sofa takes the throw off the arm and wraps it around her hips as if a skirt. Then she faces the beam of light and begins to laugh. To her joy she sees Maxine laugh also. Delighted Beth whoops with glee claps her hands and stamps her feet as she begins their dance. Her eyes never leave Maxine's.

Then to Beth's amazement Maxine begins her own dance within the beam of light moving close to the edge of the table. Though afraid the image will disappear Beth inches up to the table. Soon the two are dancing in sync to music only they hear, music filled with love and joyful laughter. As they move the storm whips around the outside of the cabin causing the floor to shudder. Beth is too entranced to feel anything but the beating of her own heart. For hours the women dance in the final fury of their love until dawn and as the sun rises Maxine slowly fades from sight. At the last moment Beth hears Maxine's voice. *My love is with you always. You are much more than you now know. Watch for your others. They are near. Before the solstice comes you will meet them and a child will seek you out. She needs your strength. Now I must go. Know that I love you and I kiss your lips forever.*

CHAPTER SIX

JUNE 10th

ELIZA

ELIZA has just finished her lunch and is putting the dishes in the dishwasher when there is a pounding on the front door. Then the doorbell chimes twice. When more pounding begins Eliza moves quickly through the house to the door and shouts, "Who the hell is there and what do you want?"

"Mrs. Staples? Eliza? It's Sheriff Frank Gilbert from Hood River. Would you open the door? I need to talk to you."

Now it begins. I know nothing, nothing, she tells herself as she turns the bolt and lets the heavy carved door swing open. Frank Gilbert former classmate of Jack's and for the past twenty years the County Sheriff at Hood River looks down at her.

Frowning up at him Eliza growls, "Frank why are you trying to kick the door down. Couldn't you just ring the bell or knock as normal people do? Why are you here anyway? You're soaked.

Come in and take that jacket off. I'll hang it in front of the fireplace." Moving into the hall ahead of him she hears the door close with a slam and turns to watch the big man lumber into the large central room where the white leather sofa sits in front of the white marble fireplace. She drapes his jacket over the ornate screen in front of the blazing fire and points to the sofa.

"Sit there. I'll get you a towel and a mug of coffee. What in the world brings you out here on a night like this?" She raises her voice as she goes into the kitchen. "Sorry I can't hear you in here. Wait till I get back with the coffee then we'll talk."

When she returns to where he sits on the sofa she tosses him a large towel and sets a mug of coffee on the table in front of him. "Drink while it's hot. It'll warm you up. I assumed you still take three spoons of sugar with cream. Was I right?"

"Yeah Eliza, that's fine." Frank Gilbert nods. "Thanks. Now sit down with me and let me tell you why I'm here. It's serious Eliza I wouldn't come all this way on a lark."

"My God, Frank stop being so mysterious. Blurt it out. You're giving me chills." Eliza shivers visibly and hugs her shoulders. "I know it has to be terrible. Why else would you be here? Did the company burn down or the mansion? Did Jack get in another accident? It's OK, Frank. Tell me. I'm not going to go to pieces. I'm a strong lady."

Taking a deep breath Gilbert sighs. "Hell there's no easy way to say this Eliza. Jack's dead. Lupe' your housekeeper found him this morning."

"Jack's dead? Did he fall down the stairs drunk again?" Eliza chokes out a half laugh then sobs. "For God sakes Frank spit it out. Tell me what happened." Tears spill down her cheeks. "Shit I've hated that sorry son of a bitch for the past twenty years and now I'm crying over his puny ass. Go figure."

"Eliza not another word till I finish. First off it was no accident. It was murder. Someone came to your house and killed him. Shot him three times. He weren't alone. A woman was with him. Peg Hartman. She's a friend of yours right? Hell Eliza they were doing it in your bed. That's where we found them both naked. Peg shot once in the back of her head and Jack three times. Do you understand Eliza?"

"No I don't. I don't understand. Peg is my best friend. She always told me she hated Jack. Hated the way he was with all those women. Especially hated what he did to me. Why were they killed in my bedroom Frank? She couldn't stand to be in the same room with him. Dear God. Does Mike Hartman know? He's down in South America this time of year on a sales trip. He's our best salesperson. Have you told him? Was it a robbery?" Suddenly Eliza stops talking and gasps for breath as shaking overcomes her.

Frank Gilbert quickly opens the wool throw beside him on the sofa and lays it gently across Eliza's shoulders. "Looks like a contract killing. Was Jack gambling again? Know he had a big a problem last year when he got pretty deep in Vegas. Did he owe big time again?"

Her eyes open wide at Gilbert's remark and she exclaims, "What gambling? I never heard about any gambling last year or any year. Are you sure about this? That damn bastard! No wonder he was always pawing around the company's accounts."

"You mean you didn't know the close call he had last year? Guess it's time you did. Story he told was he lost a million of a casino's money then left Vegas before he paid back. Remember the crash he had? Weren't any accident. A couple of toughs sent by Vegas to collect found him then took him for a late night ride. He sold his stock in Staples Packing Company to you didn't he? Said he had to as he needed cash fast. Sure you didn't know?"

"He asked for money to invest in some company. He didn't own any shares to sell. I gave him a large sum to get him off the Company's accounts. He told me it was for a business venture that eventually fell through and I had to put him back on salary afterwards." Eliza laughs a bit too loudly and shakes her head. "Good lord poor old Jack what an idiot. No wonder he kept whining about his salary being too low. He really didn't have any money. Damn. That's too funny for words."

She pauses frowning at Gilbert. "But you knew him Frank. You were his best friend. You had to know Jack was in deep. Why didn't you tell me? You knew he would never tell me. As his friend you should have told me. We could have gotten him help. We'd been nothing to each other for the last twenty years but I would have helped him. I was never surprised at anything Jack did. Not really surprised now when you tell me he took his woman to my bed. That's Jack. Peg? Peg shocks me. Why would she get involved with him? Did she gamble too?"

"Not that we know Eliza. Frank got too wild and crazy so I never hung with him much anymore. Got a great wife and wouldn't hurt her for the world. Yeah I cared for Jack. He was like a brother growing up. Still was off and on." Frank paused and stared at the floor. "Just a shit way to go that's what I say. A real shit way to go."

Neither speaks for several minutes as they sip from their mugs and stare at the flames in the fireplace. Finally Frank clears his throat. "Sorry Eliza got lost for a moment. Hell, enough of this. Let me finish about the house. Nothing seems out of place. There were clothes scattered everywhere and a suitcase in the entry. You'll have to tell if anything's missing. Don't look so but till you see it we won't know for certain.

"Here's what we think happened," he continues. "Jack and Peg came to the mansion in his Mercedes. Got passionate and began to undress in the car. Then they moved into the doorway of the house and up the stairs. Seems Jack opened the door and turned off the alarm. A bottle of champagne and two glasses were by the bed. We found the cork in the kitchen sink wrapped in a towel. A door of the glass cabinet was open. We figure at some time he came downstairs to get wine and glasses and took them back up.

"The front door was open when Lupe' got back from her vacation. Jack paid for it so she says. Now I'm guessing here he wanted to make certain she wouldn't catch him and Peg in the act. That last is my opinion from what Lupe' told me. Like I said the alarm was off. We figure it made easy entry for whoever did the job. Lupe' took it real hard and is still in the hospital sedated. She'd like you to come see her when you come back. I told her I'd give you the message. It's a hell of a puzzle Eliza a hell of a mess. Gee whiz the town never had such a scandal. Most figured Jack would be killed by a cuckolded hubby. It's Peg that's stunned us all. Jack's sure pushed both ends to the middle always did.

"Need you to come back to get things settled Eliza. Need your fingerprints to check off from those we found. And a statement on when you last saw him. Everyone who knew him is doing this. Mike Hartman will do this when we find him. Could you come with me now tonight?"

"Not tonight. I'm not driving to Hood River tonight. Not in this weather. For heaven's sakes Frank let me have at least one night to take this in. Jack wasn't much of a husband but we stayed together for over thirty years. Let me have a while to absorb all this. No I'm not going with you tonight. I'll come tomorrow. Yes that's what I'll do. I'll come sometime tomorrow. Not early maybe not till late afternoon. I need to make calls tonight. Need to call Dana and Mike and Lupe' and our lawyer and the company board. I'll come but not now. Just go away Frank. I want to be alone. Just go away."

"Don't know if I should leave you here Eliza hate for you to drive yourself."

"Frank I will drive over tomorrow. Not tonight. Do you hear me? This has really shaken me. I'm sickened by it and terribly sad. Right now I want to lie down. Please go away. I need to make sense out of this mess. How could Peg betray me and what about all these years being close friends? She was my best friend. How could she be with Jack?"

Eliza stands up and takes both mugs to the kitchen sink. Then she returns to take Frank's half dried jacket from the screen and holds it out for him to take. "I got reports to make so you get a glass and hold it with both hands. That way forensics can start fingerprinting early a.m. You can't go to the mansion though. It's sealed. You need anything I go with you. Sorry. That's the way it's got to be."

"Then you'll do it Frank. There are only a few things I want from the house. You can send someone over to bag Jack's personal items from the drawers and closets and give them to Goodwill or put them in the den downstairs. Have someone you trust do it. I'll pay for their services. I'll empty the safe when you and I go there in a day or so.

"Also take the bed and bedding out of the room as soon as you can. Dispose of it or put it wherever you want. Then have the rugs and other furniture removed. Give them to whoever wants them if they're not bloody. Finally lock the room. The key is on a hook along the top inside the room. Don't tell me it isn't your job Frank. As Jack's friend knowing what you did and didn't do you owe us this and much more. Damn it! Why couldn't Jack have gotten himself killed outside the house?"

CHAPTER SEVEN

JUNE 15th

LIZ

LIZ moves within the paradox Peter's death brought to her. The two women come to the tables in her dining room every day irritate her as much as they tantalize her. There seems to be no way to make contact with them. Each comes into the room then leaves at no special time and for no apparent reason. She sees them both in the room more often in the evening though each shows no sign that the other is near her.

The more Liz sees them the more she realizes that except for the length of their hair they look exactly as twins and again exactly as she does. Liz wishes that Alex were back at Redcliff's Beach. "What did Peter say to Alex that would cause her to run away? I miss her. I know he said not to trust her yet there's no one else who saw him within he beam of light and maybe help me understand this whole thing."

Looking out the north windows toward Alex's house she knows the Alex of years past would be here wanting to talk about every little nuance of what the women are doing. Peter's warning about Alex continues to buzz around her head and she realizes she is a bit frightened but mostly she wonders what Peter had said that made Alex flee right after she saw him in the beam of light. If she is one of the great clairvoyants as she claims to be why miss this opportunity to watch the two women, the old Alex would never have left Liz's house.

Liz studies Alex's house over the grass-topped dunes and sees deck furniture sitting where it usually does though a couple of lounge pads have been blown off the deck. "I'll go over later and tuck all of them under the south overhang. Damn it Alex what are you up to now? The last time you left in the same huff was the time I tried to fix you up with Bob Drake. You took one look at him and fled. Bob didn't stay either. You disappeared for weeks. Come to think of it you didn't explain where you went that time either."

Turning from the window Liz nearly walks into a woman walking into the room through a set of open French doors. She passes Liz then goes back to close the doors. When the woman again passes her Liz touches the woman's shoulder. "Hello there. I am Liz Day. I believe we were both Elizabeth Ann Anderson when we were children and came here to our father's cabin every summer. Do you realize you are in my home as well as your own?"

Gasping the woman looks wildly around the room before she sees Liz standing beside her. Pushing Liz's hand off her arm the woman reopens the French door and runs onto her deck. Liz's reaction is to hurry after the woman yet when she reaches where the open French door had been she finds herself in front of her own slider doors. Both the woman and the French doors are gone. Stunned Liz backs up to her dining table and sits staring at where the woman vanished.

Slowly the set of French doors reappears and the woman walks inside looking wildly around the room. This time Liz stays at the table and talks softly to the woman. "I'm here at the table. You are by your own French doors and if you'll look to your left you'll see me sitting at my own dining table which you can see is somehow joined with yours. Please look at me. I am Elizabeth Anderson Day. Liz Day. My home is within the same space where your home sits on Redcliff's Beach. Were you called Elizabeth Ann Anderson when you were a child? Did you come to your father's cabin every summer?"

The woman looks toward her own dining table then a frown twists her face as she stares at Liz. "Who the hell are you and why are you here? I want you out of my home. Get out now." As she speaks she walks across the room towards Liz. As she reaches out to touch Liz, her face changes to absolute shock and she runs into her spacious kitchen. Liz tries to follow yet is stopped by her own kitchen's counters and the woman's home vanishes.

Liz waits at her own table hoping the woman will return and several minutes later the woman reappears in the corner of Liz's dining room and goes quickly out the same set of French doors as before. Liz feels the air move as the woman moves out the doors. "How amazing you are. We could be twins. Do you know there is another of us also living within this space?" Liz whispers as she walks out her own slider and crosses her deck to where the woman stands leaning at another deck railing. Liz touches the woman's shoulder. "Hello? I'm beside you again. I believe you heard me ask if you are Elizabeth Ann Anderson. I am also."

This time the woman looks Liz directly in her eyes. She studies Liz very carefully before answering, "Yes I was Elizabeth Ann Anderson before I married. Now I'm called Eliza Staples. You can't be the Elizabeth Ann Anderson you say stayed summers here at a cabin my father built. I am. So what I want to know is who the hell are you and why do you keep popping into my life?"

"We live in spaces where each of our homes exist Eliza. I don't know why, we just do. My name is Liz Day. I've lived at Redcliff's for most of my life in the remodeled home where my father built his cabin when I was a child. I believe you and I are part of a phenomenon where three Elizabeth Ann Andersons somehow live in the same space yet in separate dimensions. The three of us look exactly alike and we've come in and out of each other's homes every day and night since June first. My husband Peter died in a plane crash on that date. Did yours die on that date?"

When Liz asks her last question the woman frowns and moves away. Liz moves with her, "My husband Peter Day died the first of June in a plane crash. Did you lose a tall dark man on that date? I saw him with Peter in the beam of light. He was very angry wasn't he? I can see your home is huge compared to mine. Yet the other of us has a cabin that looks the same as the one my dad built. Somehow we are of each other and come from the same parents. Stay with me and sit at your table and talk with me. Tell me about yourself. Please? Don't leave me."

As Liz's words rush out the woman stares at her with a stunned expression until the vision of the angry man is mentioned. Then she raises her arms and tries to push Liz away. "Get away from me. Get away from me. You're not real. You don't exist. Go away. Go away!" Flailing her arms in frantic gestures the woman swings at Liz then disappears through her French door.

"No. Don't go. Please stay. We have to talk. We must be of the same person. We both live within this place at Redcliff's. I have a sister named Dana. Do you?" Tears run down Liz's cheeks as she goes back into her own home and closes the open slider door behind her. The scene spins in her head until the whole thing becomes ludicrous and she begins to laugh. "Oh double shit, that poor woman must think she's gone nuts. Damn I wish Alex was here. I need someone to talk to about these damn women."

Again Peter's warning comes to her. "What did he mean Alex isn't who I think she is? How could she be my enemy? Why wasn't he clearer? I've known her for years and really only know what she told us about being a Russian ballerina and clairvoyant. Nobody ever challenged her story that I know. Peter did laugh at her but not with any humor. He never liked my being with her especially when he traveled. He didn't understand how much I needed her friendship. It was too lonely when he was gone and Alex was always there for me to talk with. Maybe I was too bedazzled by her exotic looks and worldly stories.

"The one time I teased Peter that he'd better not run away with her he got very angry. Told me he'd rather kiss a snake. Seeing my shocked reaction he laughed as if he'd made the best joke. Then he grabbed me and nuzzled my neck saying, 'I never liked wild meat. Give me a tender-breasted chicken with great legs and thighs.' Good thing I loved him so much as that was a terrible backhanded compliment."

Liz stares at the tables where she often sees the other women sitting at but never when she is there. Realizing nothing can be done about either Alex or the women she shakes off the thoughts and scolds herself. "It's time to tackle Peter's office. Has to be done sometime and the sooner the better. Get the company papers for Bob Drake and clear out the rest. It's a great room and I might as well start using it as my own space and turn my office into a guest room."

As she talks to herself she goes to the pantry and pulls out large grocery sacks. Then she stops with a shudder. "Jeepers this makes Peter being gone so final. Oh hell what's got to be done must be done. Big question is what to keep?" Taking one of the marking pens from a kitchen drawer she pens a word across each sack: BOB, PERSONAL, TOSS, KEEP. Then she carries the sacks to Peter's office door and pushes down on the brass lever to open the heavy oak door. Nothing happens. The door stays firmly shut. She presses the lever again and again nothing happens. Then slapping her forehead Liz laughs. "Of course Peter always locked the door when he went out of town or we had visitors. Now where is the key? He told me one that the best hiding places are always in plain sight."

Chuckling as she walks to the kitchen door to stand before a row of pegs with several jackets hanging from them. Lifting each jacket off each peg, Liz finds one peg with several key rings holding several types of keys. Liz laughs. "Well Peter, they're in plain sight but which of these things holds the keys I need?" Pulling the key rings off the peg she spreads them across the counter and through the process of elimination finally finds the ones she needs. They're an odd set of two tubular keys attached together by a strong clip. Both keys are different sizes yet both have five facets down their tubular length. Taking these back to the office door she fits the larger key into the lock on the lever. Then only after turning the key five times making as many clicks does the door swing wide open without assistance.

Startled Liz jumps away and stares at the door for several seconds before pushing it wide open. Walking slowly to the large mahogany desk in the center of the room she feels as if an intruder in Peter's private space. Shaking her head she scolds herself. "Good grief, don't be so damned silly. We were married for thirty years. He locked the door against unknown people not me."

Still she returns to the open door and closes it as Peter would have done. Staring at the desk, Liz shivers. "Okay, take a deep breath and go for it. Let's see what Peter's been hiding all these years." Though she said the words in jest it seems the words hang in the room for several seconds. Then she tosses the sacks onto the floor and pulls Peter's oversized leather swivel chair out from the desk and sinks into it. Immediately she pulls open the middle drawer. A thin laptop computer with a leather-bound logbook/calendar under it lies in the very center of the drawer. To the right sits a cell phone and a rather large badge on a long leather neck strap. The front of the badge shows Peter's face and a thumb print. She reads his name and the words under it. "Peter Day, WCA." Turning the badge over she sees strips of colors with a photo of his eye but nothing more to tell her why he had it. Deciding it was left over from one of his trips she drops it back onto the laptop and closes the drawer.

The top right drawer opens smoothly revealing office supplies. The deep drawer under that holds tax files, investment information, and a manila envelope labeled: COPIES OF WILLS. Seeing the words Liz remembers the day Peter took her to meet Bob Drake and sign the wills. It was Bob Drake who Liz called first to tell of the plane crash. That evening he'd flown his own plane over to be with her and to read Peter's Will to her. As executor Bob followed Peter's instructions clearing all debts notifying those who needed to be informed and sent out death certificates where needed. He was Peter's best friend and a good friend to her. Since Peter's death Bob had finalized the sale of their business then suggested investments that would continue to allow her to be independent of money worries. As Liz closes the drawer she feels pleased her future is now so secure.

Turning to the deep drawer on the left side of the desk she pulls on the handle. It doesn't move. Liz pushes the chair away and tries to pull the drawer straight out. Still it doesn't move. Finally she kneels in front of the drawer and checks the handle. On this close inspection she sees a small keyhole under the handle that can't be seen when sitting upright. Taking the set of keys off the desk she takes the smaller key with five ridges around the tubular form and inserts it into the lock. Again she needs to turn the key until all five ridges are inside the lock.

When it doesn't open at that point, Liz continues to turn the key five more times and with each turn she hears five distinct clicks. At that time the drawer slides open with a soft buzzing sound.

Liz can only stare at the contents in the drawer for several minutes. Then she slowly sits on the chair and studies the several large manila envelopes standing upright at the front of the drawer. Behind these are two metal boxes, a smaller one on top of a larger one. Slowly Liz pulls out each envelope and places them on the left side of the wide desk. Then she lifts the smaller box out and sets it to her right and puts the larger box directly in front of her. "Well well, Peter Day. What have we here? What have you been up to these many years?" Suddenly Liz recalls headlines about wonderful community leaders being exposed of their hidden addictions after their deaths. She groans. "Oh please dear God, please don't let him have been a porno king or anything sinister."

As it looks somehow less ominous she tackles the smaller box first. Cautiously she picks it up and shakes it gently. The sound from inside is dull like paper items or something soft. "Where's the key to these? Do I even need one? They look like the same boxes you can get at any store in the mall. A flat-headed screwdriver and a hammer should be all I need for this job."

Hurrying into the kitchen she grabs her small tool kit from under the sink. The one Peter bought for her their second Christmas. He had laughed when she'd asked for it but now she couldn't count the times she'd used one or more of the tools. Taking the screwdriver and hammer with her she almost runs back to Peter's desk and again closes the office door behind her. Laying the box on its side she wedges the driver into the space next to the lock. Then she pounds the hammer down and drives the screwdriver into the box and twists until the lid pops open. Inside are several passports. She picks up each and opens it only to see Peter's face on it with a different name and address. There are seven passports all well used and up to date each with a different name and address.

"Peter what the hell is this?" Liz spits as she pushes the box away and stares at what she's found. Tears slip down her cheeks as she again picks up each passport opens it and thumbs through the pages. A deep aching fear begins in the pit of her stomach. "Oh, Peter. Who were you? What did you really do for a living? Why would you ever need all of these?"

Returning the passports to the box she pushes it away and turns her attention to the larger box. Again she uses the screwdriver and hammer to open it and again there are more passports for several countries. These are wrapped together by thick rubber bands around stacks of currency for each country indicated in the passport. Placing the envelopes back into the large box she returns both boxes and manila envelopes to the drawer and is about to close it when she notices this drawer is half as deep as the desk. Pushing the drawer almost closed Liz stands in front of it and with both hands pulls the drawer with a yank. There is a hard bump before it slides past where it had stopped before and the drawer slides out another two feet.

The exposed drawer makes Liz gasp when she sees it is stuffed with bundles of one hundred dollar bills. Dumbfounded Liz can only sit and stare at the find. Finally after several minutes she picks one bundle up and counts each bill discovering there are one hundred bills in each bundle and over one hundred bundles. Quickly assessing the contents she realizes the box holds more than a million dollars.

A sudden laugh erupts from her throat and Liz raises both her hands over her head and shouts, "I don't know how you got this loot Peter but I'm not giving it to Bob! He's going to have to ask for it. There are a lot of things I can use this money for rather than giving it back to the company's accounts." Taking two of the grocery sacks she stuffs one inside the other and begins to fill the doubled bag with the bundles of money.

When the bag is full she carries it into her pantry. Walking directly to the chest-style freezer sitting at the back wall she lifts the freezer lid then moves baskets of frozen vegetables and meats off to one side. When she clears a space at the very bottom of the freezer she sets the sack of money into it. Then she methodically restacks the baskets of frozen food to cover it.

When she is done there is one empty freezer basket that had been where the bag of money is now. Setting the basket on the floor Liz quickly fills it with several small items off the pantry shelves then she sets it on the shelf space where the food items had been. Laughing Liz looks up and shakes her fist over her head, "I've done it Peter. I've hid the money in plain sight. Now we'll see if Bob knows about it. If he does he'll ask for it. If not it's mine to do with as I want."

After shutting the freezer lid, Liz gives it a pat then returns to Peter's office. Going back to the desk she begins to push the drawer closed. Instead she stops and reaches to touch the manila envelopes. As she does fear of what she might find causes her to quickly close and lock the drawer. Then she drops the keys into the top drawer thinking about what she had found. A deep sadness sweeps over Liz as she doesn't know what to do next. Only a few jobs could require such items and that thought frightens her very much.

At that moment the phone on the desk rings. Liz lets it ring several times before she picks up the receiver. It's Bob Drake. "Stay in the house lock the doors speak to no one on the phone or otherwise. Not anyone. Understand?"

"Yes Bob. Will you tell me the truth?"

"Much as I can Liz much as allowed."

CHAPTER EIGHT

JUNE 15th

BETH

BETH is thrown out of bed by the force of the first huge wave that hits her cabin. Dazed she sits on the floor for almost a minute trying to understand what she'd been dreaming to cause such a reaction. When the second wave hits the cabin she scrambles back onto her bed and pulls the quilt over her head.

She cringes as wind screams around the south corner of her bedroom. It is the third wave that rocks the cabin causing the window on the south wall to crack and is the catalyst that propels Beth from the bed into her warmest clothes and boots.

Rushing into the hall she sees floater logs sticking though shattered windows and shutters along the north wall. A shorter log rolls across the kitchen floor and she hears the sounds of shattering glass where the slider doors had been. Flinging the hall closet door open she grabs two large metal boxes containing her personal and financial information and then grabs her purse off a peg next to the front door as she rushes into the carport where she throws boxes and her purse into the pickup truck. For once she is relieved she left the keys in the ignition.

Starting the motor she backs the vehicle up the driveway and turns it south onto Shoreline Drive. For several seconds she watches the waves batter her small cabin and is undecided whether to flee or to stay and watch its destruction. Jagged streaks of lightning illuminate the scene to reveal the last low sand dunes north of her place being flattened.

"Damn, damn, damn. This is a bad one Max. This is it. The cabin will go this time. Wash away like the others did forty years ago. Oh no Max I forgot the photos of our life. I can't lose you again, never again."

Pushing against the wind she opens the truck door then struggles to walk upright to the carport. Then she's through the front door of the cabin grabbing framed photos off walls and photo albums off bookshelves and pushing all of them into a wheeled duffle bag she pulled from the hall closet. Wrenching the heavy duffle bag to the front door Beth pushes it through the door as a strong gust shakes the cabin. Stumbling Beth smacks her head on the door frame.

The strong wind helps push her back to the truck however she is unable to open the truck's door against these same winds. Finally there is a lull in the gusts letting her open the truck door and push the heavy bag onto the passenger seat. Then she falls into the driver's seat and the wind slams the truck's door shut behind her. For several seconds Beth tries to decide whether to stay or leave when the decision is made for her as the blow on her head takes over and she falls into a deep sleep.

The next morning when the sun rises over the coastal mountain range and warms her face Beth slowly awakens. At first she is puzzled as to where she is or why her head pounds on the left side of her forehead. When she touches where it hurts she feels a large rounded bump. "What happened to me? Why am I out here? Why the hell am I in the truck and sitting on Shoreline Road? Why does my head hurt so much?"

As she tries to sit upright her head spins and she lays her head back against the seat. Looking down to the cabin she sees large logs lying halfway across her driveway. The logs jog her memory and bit by bit Beth remembers the events of the night before: the waves, the wind, the truck, the photos, and even the blow to her head.

"Maxine I hate saying this but I doubt I could have saved you if you'd been here. It's almost a blessing you died before this horrible storm tore through our cabin. I don't know if the cabin is sturdy enough for me to walk through it. I doubt I can stay here any longer. Thank God I saved our photos Max. I saved you and me together, our life together." Shattered by both relief and grief Beth sobs.

Leaving the truck where it is, Beth walks down the graveled drive to the first float log blocking her way and weaves her way through the debris piled in the front of the carport. The cabin's front door hangs from one hinge so Beth pushes it wider then props it open. Slipping into the hallway she sees that both the bathroom and guest room doors are shut tight. Opening the first she finds the room is clean except for a bit of wet sand washed across the tiled floor. Then Beth opens the guestroom door to find this room is dry and even cleaner. That the storm missed those windows Beth feels is a miracle as she sees they are still covered by their shutters and all the panes have their glass.

Turning back into the hallway she looks past her bedroom door and sees the main devastation in the cabin. Long logs lie across the floor where the hospital bed had sat only days before. Shorter logs are piled against these. More long logs protrude into the room through shattered windows and others go out through the glassless slider door openings. Smashed bookcases and other items are scattered everywhere. Besides the logs the floor is covered with piles of sand, flotsam and shattered glass.

In the kitchen the debris is piled so high it buries the counter tops and spills out the open places where windows used to be. The high cabinet doors are closed and when Beth is finally able to clear one and is relieved to find the items inside clean and dry. The yacht-quality cabinetry her father built saved the kitchen. "Thank you Daddy. Thank you for expecting the worst storm ever and building the cabin to handle it."

Finally Beth goes to her bedroom door. It is shut tight and she holds her breath when she pulls it open then shouts with relief, "It's as I left it! The wind must have slammed the door shut. There's a bit of sand but I think it's less than in the bathroom. That cracked window didn't even blow out. This is an easy fix. If the cabin can survive this storm so can I. Let's get help. Got to call my insurance guy he'll know what to do first."

Lifting the receiver off the phone on the nightstand she gets a dial tone and tears fill her eyes as she gives thanks. Thumbing through the phone book from the night stand drawer she finds the man's number and calls. When George Ames answers Beth quickly fills him in on what has happened. He tells her not to move anything though she can start making a list of what she knows is missing from the cabin and what is damaged. He will be there within the hour. Beth thanks him and hangs up. Then she sits on the edge of her bed and whispers, "I'm not alone Max. Ames said he knows others who can put the cabin right again. Maybe it will survive. Maybe I will."

A while after her call to him Ames arrives at the cabin and tells her, "Your beach was hit the worst. There's a bit of debris on the highway near Pacific Beach but it missed Ocean Shores completely. Now let's see that list you started and we'll walk through the house together. You ready?"

Beth nods as she hands over her writing pad and follows him into the main room as far as they can go. Ames asks questions then makes notes of her replies and adds to the list items she had not thought damaged. When he is done with the inside they go out to the front drive to study the damage around the outside of the cabin. "I'll give you good news first. Those logs stuck through the front room windows can be used to rebuild the frontage along the north side of the cabin and protect the deck from future storms. That should really cut the cost. Your dad did a great job on the original construction anchoring those steel under beams to the bedrock on this high point. They held it together.

"The first thing to be done is to clear out the cabin. I have a crew on the way up from Hoquiam with trucks and men to shovel out the flotsam then wash off the inside. They'll leave the bedrooms and bath for you to do later as those rooms only need a good sweeping to be clean again. Everything that's electrical is damaged and will be tossed including all appliances. Saltwater and sand ruin electrical wiring and that will all have to be redone right after the clean up.

"My brother Tom owns heavy equipment and builds bulkheads and decks. He's between jobs so he'll be here around the same time the cleanup crew is. So stay close until they both come as you have to sign both work orders or nothing will happen. Don't worry. Your home should be back to normal within the week. Once you've signed their work orders they will want you out of the way. Go comb the south beach for your things before another high tide pulls them out to sea. You'll be surprised what you'll find that can be saved."

After thanking Ames Beth watches his car vanish down Ocean Shores Drive then she turns to look at her cabin. Tears roll down her cheeks as she hugs herself. From that angle the cabin appears only slightly damaged. "I think we got a pass on this one Max. It sounds as if the cabin is as shipshape as Dad wanted it to be. Maybe I'll get to stay here for a few more years after all."

After Beth lifts the long beach wagon off the hook it's hung from for years, she pulls it down to the beach. Grinning, she looks up at the now blue sky. "You know God, when I asked for something to get me through the next months I should have been more specific. I didn't mean being trashed by one of your perfect storms."

CHAPTER NINE

JUNE 15

ELIZA

ELIZA smells the aroma of fresh coffee before she sees the red light showing it has finished brewing. She crosses the wide floor of the widows walk and pushes her coffee mug under the spigot adding cream to the mug as it fills. She's so glad to be home again and enjoying the view and gadgets Dana and she had found to add to this wonderful third floor. Taking the mug over to a high backed wicker chair facing the ocean she studies the full seven-mile length of Redcliff's Beach. Everywhere she looks the beach is awash with kids, kites, dogs, beachcombers, and joggers. Feeling her cell phone vibrate in the pocket of her robe she answers it and is very pleased to hear her sister Dana's voice.

"Well good morning. I'm up in the widow's walk enjoying the view and thinking of how lovely it is to have the mini kitchen you insisted on putting up here. You need to be here with me. When is that house of yours getting sold?"

Dana laughs, "That's why I called, sis. It looks as if I have a buyer for my house and if things go well it should close within the month. I've already talked to a couple of movers to get estimates. I was wondering how the last day at the Grand Jury went for you. Did they come to a defining decision?"

"No. The Jury ended the last day without any charges being made. My lawyer said that happens more often than most people would think. Thanks again for letting me stay at your place all week. That made the trip almost enjoyable. Is there anything I can do for you at this end?"

"Not really. I'm coming up next week to recheck the measurements of my rooms and see if I remember correctly the exact layout. I don't want to haul up a lot of unnecessary furniture and stuff. How was your trip home?"

"It's great to be back at Redcliff's that's for sure. As for the things you want to bring here really think about what is important to you as you may want to buy new things to fit into your new life up here. I'd love helping you shop as you did for me and now that I've lived here a while I can see we need more to fill the common rooms. Right now it looks a bit like a concert hall. Maybe a few more overstuffed chairs but we can discuss that after you move here. It's going to be so great having you here."

When the sisters say their goodbyes Eliza takes her empty mug to the small sink by the coffee maker, washes and sets it in the drainer to dry. Then she goes down to her bedroom and dresses before going down to the first floor. Walking to the French doors she opens one and leans on the door frame. Looking north to the red cliffs she sees that end of the beach looks as if an ant's nest has been stirred up.

Eliza smiles at how good it is to be back at Redcliff's. Her mind races back over days of the Grand Jury. She wonders why the alibi Al and Penny gave her held firm just as Mike Hartman's alibi fell apart. He told of going to Chili as planned then after completing his work there he flew to New York City to be with a woman he'd met a few years before. He claimed he was with her there when the murders happened and when he saw a report on CNN news he called Sheriff Gilbert then flew home to Hood River. The Sheriff interviewed him over the phone and again when Mike got home.

Even then the Sheriff called the woman to check out Mike's story and she confirmed Mike's statement. Then she added her plans to divorce her husband so she and Mike could marry. Because of part of her statement the woman had to fly out to swear that Mike's statement was true and that he had not asked her to marry him.

Eliza smiles as she remembers how the woman's testimony hurt Mike more than it helped him no matter how she reassured the Jury she was telling the truth. Seems half the town is positive I killed Jack and the other half thinks Mike Hartman did it. After all the evidence was presented the coroner announced the jury's decision that Jack was murdered by person or persons unknown. When he said that the whole room laughed though I sobbed for several minutes stunning the crowd and shocking me.

"I'll admit it I loved the guy at the beginning and even some till the end. He broke my heart in a thousand ways yet I almost regret killing him. Not about killing Peg though. She deserved it. She lied to me over and over. Said she was my friend and hated Jack. His betrayal I got used to years ago but not hers ever."

Not realizing her complete change of heart about the two people she's killed Eliza feels righteous in shooting Peg Hartman. "She was my friend for as long as I can remember. How could she have done that to me? Though Mike looked sad I didn't say a word to him. What was there to say? His wife was killed with her head in my husband's crotch. There's nothing to add to that."

As Eliza walks out to her deck railing a voice asks, "Are you Elizabeth Ann Anderson?"

Turning to her left Eliza sees a woman moving towards her. "Well, yes, I was. Actually I'm Eliza Staples. But who the hell are you? How did you get into my house and what are you doing here?"

The woman continues to come closer telling her they are of three women who look alike and live within her father's cabin space with Eliza's house being the largest. This woman claims her house fits inside hers while the family cabin fits inside the woman's. Eliza backs away as the woman as she speaks of the death of her husband on June first and then asks if a loved one of Eliza's died that day.

Panic overwhelms Eliza and she screams, "Get away from me... Still the woman walks toward her telling her about their being from one Elizabeth Ann Anderson. As the woman reaches out to touch her shoulder Eliza swings a fist to hit her and the woman disappears. Completely confused Eliza flees across her deck and down to the path through the high dunes. When she stops at the edge of the outgoing tide and looks back there is no other woman on her deck or in the doorway nor has anyone followed her onto the beach.

Shaking Eliza feels nauseous as she plods home through deep sand on the path and mutters, "I must be going mad. Killing Jack has turned my life upside down. Dear God how do I ever come back from this horrible thing I've done?"

At the bottom step to her deck she sees the French doors are still open so she advances cautiously to them and peers into her house. No one is there. At least the other woman is nowhere to be seen. Still Eliza feels very anxious and she searches through the large house checking each room to make certain the house is empty.

Going into her kitchen Eliza opens the fridge and pulls sandwich fixings off the shelves then closes the door. As she does she thinks over what happened and laughs. "How weird was that? Who will ever believe what I just saw. Now that I think about her the woman did look familiar to me. Where did she come from? More importantly where did she go?"

Her mind whirs with possibilities as she takes the sandwich and a bottle of beer out to the deck and settles into one of the chaise lounges. "Seeing that woman is almost too much. I must remember that I'm under a lot of stress and must stay calm. Most of all I must stop talking to myself."

When the sandwich is eaten Eliza lets the sun's warmth relax her and closes her eyes. Listening to the sounds off the beach she falls into a half sleep. Until she realizes the footsteps she hears are close by and they are crossing her deck. Sitting up she looks to where her French doors should be she sees a woman much the same as the last woman walk to the edge of a de-railed deck then jump off onto the sand.

Swinging her feet off the lounge, Eliza shouts, "Stop! You there stop right there. What were you doing in my house? Who are you?" The woman does not respond but stops at a wagon sitting there and walks down the beach. Stunned Eliza watches the woman crisscross a flat beach empty of people or houses or motels. There is no one on the beach besides the one woman who pokes through one pile of debris after another.

Shaking Eliza rubs her eyes and when she looks again at the south beach she is relieved to see it full of people with cabins, homes, motels, and hotels all along Shoreline Drive. The woman is nowhere to be seen. Eliza scolds herself. "Good God I'm falling apart. Is this what happens with guilt? I've got to stop thinking about that damned DA who told Mike and me to remember that murder cases never close. I practically sneered at the bastard as I told him 'Good. Maybe you'll catch the guy who did it.' I looked at Mike as I said it. To Hell with them all Jack deserved to die and I'm lucky I finally caught him when my meds were off kilter. Now I want as many good years as I lived with that asshole Jack Staples. I deserve some blessings. In fact at this moment I vow to make my own luck doing good deeds and Jack's death can be counted as the first."

CHAPTER TEN

JUNE 15th

LIZ

LIZ waits at the dining table for Bob Drake to arrive. "What is he going to tell me about Peter that I don't already know? That I was I a front, a cover, a ploy, or just a local bimbo to have a few laughs with then go on his merry way to another country and another woman over there? Dear God let me be the only one he ever loved. I can take everything else if I know that. Damn you Peter Day what have you done to me?" she hisses shaking her fist at the center of the ceiling where the beam of light had brought him back to her last week. At that moment the door bell chimes and Liz is relieved to find Bob Drake on the front stoop holding a large metal box in each hand.

Liz laughs. "Hello Bob your timing is faultless. I was coming to look for you and here you are."

The tall blonde man smiles broadly as he sets the boxes in front of Peter's office door and gives her a warm hug. "Ah Liz you are a wonder. Sorry I'm late but air traffic out of Boeing field was bad with the fog. You know how it gets."

Liz chokes out, "Yes Bob I know all about fog."

"Liz cut out my tongue. I'm sorry. I'm as much on edge as you must be so before we get to clearing out Pete's office I'd be forever grateful for a mug of java with a double of scotch to sweeten it. It's been a tough day and it's not going to get easier."

Liz leads him to the kitchen where she measures coffee into her espresso machine then pours a large measure of scotch into two mugs. She looks at him. "One jigger for me and two for you, right?"

Bob nods. "Peter taught you well old girl. Hang on to that thought as you're in for a rather rough ride. You'll come up for air soon. Just hold on tight."

When they both have their mugs of the strong brew Bob raises his and toasts, "To the oldest and dearest."

Liz touches her mug to his, "To the oldest and dearest."

Bob downs the hot drink in what appears to be one long gulp smacks his lips and sighs. "Liz you know how to reach a man's heart. Could you manage another for each of us to nurse while packing up Pete's office?"

"Sure though I'll stick to this one with a bit more lift in it." She makes another drink and hands it to him. "Here's your crutch Bob. Now I want answers, no more lies. Tell me what Peter did. Yes or no was he an agent for our government?"

Bob sips the refreshed brew and studies Liz's face for a long minute before he answers. "Peter worked for 'the company' I work for. We did not own nor work for an ordinary business. There was neither a merger nor a sale of our business. Peter wanted to retire to spend what time he had left with you at Redcliff's. All his money is legit: retirement, life insurance, and several large bonuses for work well done. Your stocks are real. Your financial status is real. Most important Liz, Peter's love for you was totally real. You were the one stable thing in his life. He loved and treasured you. We both did."

Liz's blinks back the tears before she speaks. "Thank you. I needed to know he loved me.

"That's all I can say about Peter."

"You came all this way to tell me so little?"

"I told you a whole lot Liz. You weren't to know any of this for your safety. Peter trusted you. His office was locked because of Alexandria. He worried how much she got out of you. That's why he kept you innocent about what he did. He couldn't let on how much was known about her. More importantly he didn't want you to be seen as a threat to her. Peter's love was that solid. How I envied you both. Why do you think I came to visit so often? You were my one stable thing too Liz."

Bob's confession of love for her passes without Liz's notice. Instead she asks "This job of his was why he died wasn't it? Peter didn't crash by mistake. He was too good a pilot for that to have happened. Besides he bought that very plane because it glided so perfectly without power. Somebody did bad things to him. Am I right?"

"The evidence shows that one bullet entered from the lower right side of the engine compartment cut the fuel line and jammed in one valve. He never knew what happened until it was too late. The company is tracking a suspect as we speak."

"Could that one suspect be Alexandria Petrow? She disappeared last week after she saw Peter within the beam of light."

"What did you say? Liz? What did you just say?" Bob stares at her dumbfounded. "You said Peter was in a beam of light? Liz? He was here in this room after his death after his cremation?"

"Yes Bob, Peter came back within a beam of light. He stood right over there on the dining table where the light came through the center of the ceiling. He was here for two nights then on the third he asked for Alex and I called her over to see him. She came and saw Peter within the beam of light. She also saw two others who were with him. You can ask her when you find her. Anyway she stayed and Peter talked to her. I don't know what he told her but right after he finished Alex fled from the house. I think she left Redcliff's that night. That was the last time he came to me. Before he left Peter told me never to trust her again."

Thrilled that she finally has someone to tell about the two other women she sees so often she continues. "The two women Peter brought to me come often as their lives connect with mine on this land our father bought years ago. Our homes sit within our own dimensions even though they're tied to this same space."

Bob is unable to speak for several minutes. He only stares at her open mouthed. Finally he unbuttons his jacket and fingers the holster holding a gun strapped to his left shoulder. "Damn. Damn it to hell Liz what you say is unbelievable. You think Alex is a good witness to seeing Peter after he died? Hell Liz don't you realize that Alex was probably the one who caused his death. She has always been your enemy and our country's enemy. Peter kept close to her to keep you safe. She will tell any kind of bullshit anyone wants to hear to get the information she needs to know. Your obsession with her drove Peter crazy with worry. He tried to tell you the truth after she filled you with her bullshit. You were her most gullible puppet."

He studies her face for several minutes then snaps, "Oh hell Liz. You didn't tell her I was coming over this morning did you? Please say you didn't."

Liz lowers her head and glowers at him her breath coming in angry pants. She spits her next words at him. "No Bob. I didn't tell anybody. Get it? I told you Alex fled after Peter talked to her a week ago. She hasn't come back or contacted me. I don't know where she is. Don't call me crazy because I see my others. I'm not and I do. I see the two women who Peter called my others. They come into my home often. I talked to one this morning next to the front slider door. I believe these women exist somehow within this space where my home sits. Why or how they do I don't know. But I'm telling you this when they do come through to me I will gladly share my life with them."

Suddenly Bob comes to her. "Liz you've gone through a rough time. Dam it gal get a grip on things. I think your mind's slipped a notch. Pull yourself together. You're seeing things that can't happen. People don't come back after they die. That only happens in the movies. We need to get you some counseling."

Liz opens her mouth to shout at him. Instead the look on his face strikes her funny and she laughs at him. Bob reaches out to grab her arms and she pushes him away. "Let me go Bob. I'm OK. You just looked so frigging proper. What an asshole you really are without Peter to buffer your rough edges? Don't talk to me about going to any of your damned doctors I'm the sanest person you'll ever know and a hell of a lot saner than you Bobby-boy or Peter or any of your company people.

"I'm not the one who leads a multitude of false lives. I've never had to have seven-plus passports to get around the world. You all are the ones who need help. Now get into that office and get your company crap out of my home. Anything you need take it tonight. The furniture you can get later and whatever stuff that's too big for now can be picked up then. I want you and the company out of my home and out of my life forever. Grab the boxes and unlock the door. Peter's keys are in the top drawer of his desk. Now pack it up and move it out big boy. I won't tolerate your sneering at me one more second then necessary."

Bob does as he's told and has the items she found the night before packed into the metal boxes within the hour. Before he closes the second metal box he grabs Peter's set of keys off the top of the desk and drops them into the box then locks both boxes.

Looking up at her he pauses then says, "You can quit being so angry with me, Liz. Remember I'm on your side and always will be. If I could stay the night I would. I'd like to meet your others but these things have to get back to Seattle ASAP. As his partner I'm responsible for Peter's papers getting a safe delivery. Know this Liz, I am I was and always will be your good friend and admirer. Don't close or lock this door. You may need a safe room sooner than I'm anticipating."

Liz blushes a bit from what they have both said so she quietly follows Bob out of the room. He opens the office door wide and turns the lock to ensure the door will open if needed. As he does she hears a hissing noise coming from the door jamb. "Noise filters," he says without looking at her. "They'll be turned off now. The company has taken control until all the equipment is removed."

"That's how you knew to call me last night isn't it?"

"Yes a satellite secures each connection worldwide. When this one was breached by your unlocking the door without punching in the code it flashed on a board in some hole in the ground then connected to me wherever I was. Sorry you had to see all this. It's been decided that since you found what you did you could see the rest of what's been here. Though I'm not sure what headquarters is going to do about your knowing it."

Liz's head snaps up and she stares at him. "Are you telling me I may be eliminated as I know too much? Or is it my dealings with a known enemy agent named Alexandria Petrow?"

Bob smiles. "No Liz you won't be eliminated. Those two things are bothersome though. You may be drafted to assist in capturing the same. We know Alex is now in Portland. She traveled to California when she left here and moved around doing the psychic fairs she often brags about. We also know she contacted her company overseas and told them you're an agent brought here by Peter to watch her. It seems you confirmed it when you refused her help to clear out Peter's things after his death. She felt it was odd that you didn't confide in her at that time. She's now certain you two were never married."

"You're telling me she told someone that I'm important to them? I knew nothing ever. Still don't other than what you told me and what I saw in that desk. Will she try to kill me? What am I to do? I don't play with guns or have dirty secrets. That's a game you and Peter played. Bob you've got to do something to protect me."

"That's why I'm here Liz. Getting Peter's things is a ploy to get in without anyone suspecting we know everything. There's a man in her house now waiting for her. He slipped in the day she drove off. He's someone we've watched for several years. We aren't surprised he's settled there. It's the guy she claimed as her brother a few summers back. Remember the benefactor from Austria?"

Seeing Liz's nod Bob bends and picks up the now full boxes and walks to the front door. As Liz follows him down the hallway she realizes he hasn't asked about the money she hid in the freezer and smiles. "Are you sure you got everything of 'the company's' cleared from the office? I gather you have since you left the door unlocked. Are you sure you don't want to secure it?"

"Yes to getting all the company's info and no to locking that door. You may need a safe room. Anything or anyone comes around that you don't know get in that room, close the door and turn the bolts twice on the inside. Understand? If Alex comes over or anyone unusual comes around you hit the red button on the phone. It dials and we come."

As she opens the front door he turns to her. "Things will move fast now Liz. Expect Alex back by the end of the week, no later for sure. When she calls you tell her this…"

CHAPTER ELEVEN

JUNE 15th

BETH

BETH has never been so glad to see a bunch of guys as she is to see the cleanup crew coming down the driveway later that morning. The crew's superintendent walks with her through the damage then hands her the work order for her to sign so he and his men can get on with the cleanup. By the time she is through doing that Tom Ames is parking his dump truck pulling a heavy trailer with the dozer/digger along Shoreline Drive and Beth meets him halfway up the driveway. As soon as he says Hello he begins explaining what he will be doing with the digger/dozer. "First thing we do is lift the logs out the clean up crew's way." he explains. "Then I'll move the sand from the south back to where it was under and around the base of your cabin. Then I sink logs to reinforce and level the decking and move more sand around them. We'll keep the shorter logs for bulkheads up the north beach. Those should stabilize the relocated dunes I'll move back up there. All you have to do is keep sign this work order and keep out of everyone's way for the whole day.

Nobody wants you getting crushed by a truck, dozer, or logs. Come talk to me around five or so, OK?"

So relieved to let someone take over what she sees an impossible job after she signs the work orders Beth goes into the carport and pulls a backpack and two water bottles then digs out four energy bars from a box on the highest shelf. Filling the water bottles at the faucet at the front corner of the carport, she drinks the first one down then refills it before putting both in the pack. Dodging the cleanup crew she scrambles through debris and out to jump off the slanting south side of the deck. Landing close to where she had left the beach sled she drops the pack on it and begins her trek down the beach.

As Beth pulls the sled behind her she munches one of the energy bars knowing she'll be glad she did. Looking at her watch she notes that it is only ten in the morning. "I'll hike to the south cliffs putting whatever I find on the high dry sand. Then on my way back I'll check things over and if it's salvageable I'll toss it on the sled. The sun and breeze will dry most of the things before I come back to them. It's a perfect day for a picnic at the beach."

Soon the dry sand above the high-tide line shows a trail of items she put there: books, lamps with shades or no shades, two of the four chairs to the dining table, the large wooden table she'd left on the deck, three rugs one from the living room and two from the kitchen, and one almost perfect end-table and one with a leg missing.

Best of all she found Maxine's bentwood rocker sticking out of a sand dune. Digging with a flat board she finds it sand-washed and scraped but mostly unharmed. In the same area she finds two floor lamps poking their bent shade holders out from the same dune. The shades are nowhere to be seen.

When she reaches the south cliffs the sun is high above and she knows it must be past noon. Feeling the four mile hike,

BETH

Beth sits on the sled and sips from a bottle of water while she eats another energy bar. Her stomach growls its welcome to the refreshments and she wonders how many days it will be before she can fix a real meal in her own kitchen.

Looking north she sees movement above and below the cabin. From where she sits the cabin seems high off the beach. The movement under the cabin she realizes is the dozer. Tom Ames is doing as he said and backfilling under the cabin. Along the driveway, workers are filling large trucks and dumpsters. Relief floods through her as she watches the effort. "Maybe the cabin will last another year after all."

When she empties the bottle of water she packs it away and begins the long walk north to collect the items she left on the dry sand. Whenever she stops to put an item on the long wagon she often sees others now that the sun is at a different angle. Most things are hers yet some are not. When she finds an item so ruined there is no real value she puts it back into the ocean letting the ebbing tide take it out. "Someone else will think they are treasures."

In some areas of the beach many of the things she finds are not hers and she realizes somewhere to the north are other people looking on beaches for their lost things. "I'll keep an eye on the lost and found ads or maybe I'll put one in for general stuff and where to find it. Someone may want these things."

When the wagon has all it can hold piled on it Beth heads directly to the cabin and empties it along the south side of the driveway. This is the first of four trips. Then she refills the water bottles and heads back to the beach. It is nearly five when she brings home the last load and finds the cleanup crew finishing the hosing down of the outside of the cabin. The driveway no longer has debris on or around it. The trucks with dumpsters filled high with shattered glass, shutters, flotsam, and ruined appliances are turning up onto Shoreline Drive. The last of the crew are winding hoses and packing other gear into their vans. Soon the crew honks their goodbyes and she waves. The Super starts the last truck and lets it idle as he returns to where Beth stands at the top of the driveway. He yells over the noise of the diesel engines, "Give us a call if you need anything else. Ames signed off on the work order. If you have questions call George. He'll give us a heads up to return and see what we missed. Let us know as we take pride in doing our best."

Shaking the man's hand she tells him how great his crew was. Just then another van of workers pulls out of the drive and beeps its farewell. Both Beth and the Super wave then say their own good-byes. Beth watches until the truck disappears down Ocean Shore Drive. Then she walks down the driveway and into the cabin to see if there is anything at all in her pantry she can eat.

Walking through the washed down cabin Beth hears the dozer at the front and goes onto the deck to watch Ames move tons of sand toward the north side of the cabin. Though he sees her wave he finishes moving the swell of sand to where he wants it then he steers the machine close to the front of the cabin and turns it off. Beth goes out front to greet him. He nods at Beth. "How does it look?"

"So much better than it did. Thank you for working magic."

"There's still a week's worth of work to do getting the bulkheads in place." He smiles as he leads her to the door of the cabin. "You were miles away so I signed off on the work order for the Super. His crew needed to get to another job. The paper's in one of the kitchen drawers. You look through the cabin and see if he or I missed anything. Though the cabin looks a hundred percent better with the glass and sand gone we might have missed something. Once I got the logs out of their way the crew was able to dig out the rest. I've placed several logs under the deck before dozing sand over them. That should hold the sea back for years. See where waves are swirling around out there? When I finish that dune you'll have good space between you and that eddy come the next storm. I'll be back in the morning. Is six too early?"

"The earlier the better," Beth tells him as they walk back through the carport. As he drives away in his truck, she gives a quick wave then goes back into the cabin, to the washed wet emptiness of her home. The float logs, smashed glass, piles of seaweed, and sand are gone. The place has been swept and hosed then scrubbed everywhere from the tiled floors to the cedar-lined walls and ceiling. What furniture there is has been moved to some ordinary position again. The heavy old brown leather sofa gleams from its washing and sits against the north wall where it always has. The round oak dining table and three of its eight chairs are back in the middle of the room. The kitchen counters and cabinets shine. Gaping holes where the stove and refrigerator should be shock her until she remembers the crew taking them. Checking the pantry closet she finds canned goods still on the shelves.

Opening a can of soup Beth eats it cold from the can and finds it delicious. "How amazing I'm still here and that the cabin still stands and that there's been a cleanup crew and dozer here all afternoon. Things look freshly scrubbed. How blessed I am. I was right when I told George Ames he was my miracle this morning. I'm looking at the proof."

Walking to the kitchen sink she clicks open the cabinet on the right takes out a glass and turns on the tap. The water runs clear as she fills the glass then drinks. As she does she realizes how clean the glass and cabinet is. "God bless Dad and his desire to make his cabin ship shape."

As she sets the glass on the counter she notices a sheet of paper in the corner next to the pantry door. Picking it up she reads a note from a window replacement man George Ames sent out. The man measured the openings for the windows and slider doors for their replacements and has replacements for all of them in his shop. If she calls before six that evening he can bring them out and put them in tomorrow. Rushing to her bedroom phone Beth calls the number and tells the man to bring the replacements. He tells her he'll also bring a larger crew to make certain they get the windows set by the end of the day.

Realizing the sun is getting low Beth pulls the beach sled back to the beach stopping only when she reaches where she had stopped loading the found items. Then she works steadily placing each item carefully on the beach wagon. As she does she notices incoming waves are bringing all sorts of flotsam onto the beach: books, pieces of furniture, trays, shoes, and clothing. Wading out to catch one recognized item after another she tosses each onto the high dry sand. "I'll let them dry there for the night. This is my last load till tomorrow. Got to get back to hose these and what I left along the driveway so they can dry by morning." Looking at the eastern horizon she frowns and states firmly, "It will not rain tonight."

When she is done hosing off the rescued items, Beth leaves the beach sled beside the cabin and goes inside. She is exhausted and decides to head for bed. Realizing she wants to be where she can see or hear if anyone messes around the stuff outside her cabin Beth changes into a pair of sweatpants and long sleeved T-shirt then pulls her sleeping bag from the top shelf of her closet and grabs a blanket and pillow off her bed. Returning to the main room she makes her bed on the leather sofa then gets a flashlight from the pantry and checks it to make certain it works. Finally she zips herself into her sleeping bag and turns off the flashlight.

CHAPTER TWELVE

JUNE 15th

ELIZA

ELIZA sees both the women in her home sometimes for seconds and sometimes for hours puttering around their own homes or out on their decks. This morning one of them spoke to her though she still can't believe what the woman said. As she roams restlessly through her elegant home then out to the wraparound deck Eliza wonders aloud, "They look so much like me except both are slimmer and have different length hair. The one who spoke to me has very short hair as if she'd been sheared. The one in the old cabin wears a pony tail. Why do they come here? Is it because I killed Jack and Peg?

"When the first woman told me her husband died June first and wondered if mine died that day too it spooked me so much. How did she know about Jack? She said he was an angry man. Why angry? Did the one living in the cabin also lose someone that day? Now that I've had time to see them several days it feels as if I should know them both."

"Each of their homes seems smaller than mine as the larger home fits within mine and the smaller one fits within that one. That small home looks exactly as my dad's old cabin was. I wish I'd stayed when the one called Liz tried to talk to me. Now she no longer sees me nor does the other woman. I'd love to know who they are and why they've come to me."

Eliza shakes her head as she laughs. "No I'm not crazy. At first I thought it was Jack coming back to cause problems for me. Then I realized if it were Jack he'd send a rapist-murderer. Not two gentle women, of that I'm very certain. Besides these women are exactly like me. Both look so much the same they could be twins. In fact except for my extra twenty pounds we could be triplets. We have the same nose, eyes and color of hair. When the one asked if I was Elizabeth Ann Anderson she even sounded like me. Damn why didn't I stay and question her? I was just so freaked out from that Grand Jury that I could only flee from the house."

Suddenly Eliza gasps as if seeing something wonderful. "My God I think I know what these women are. Where is that book on metaphysical events Dana gave me last Christmas? It tells about a sort of phenomenon of multiple lives. Maybe that's what this is. What was it called? Some dimension? No, some kind of lives, but what? Split dimensions? Dana loves all that stuff and goes to see people channel ancient entities who take over their bodies. Where is that book? I know I didn't dump it before the move in."

As she talks to herself she runs a finger over the spines of the books on shelves covering the walls on either side of the high stone fireplace then down the hallway into the entry. "Dana tried to get me to go to those readings she loved so much. When I wouldn't go she got her friends to go with her. Aha here it is." Pulling a large book off the shelf Eliza carries it to the dining table where she opens it and scans the table of contents.

"Yes here it is. Parallel Lives (PL). That's what we three women must be… Yes! Here it is, 'These lives split from an Original Life entity to form another life within a parallel dimension. It is felt these lives happen when the Original Life (OL) is traumatized by an abrupt life change not of his choosing therefore compelling the OL to form a new life. It is supposed that the trauma causes an energy break within the OL with such great intensity the PL is created in another dimension. At that time the OL continues to exist within its dimension unaware of the new PL life formed. Within this parallel dimension the PL lives to continue their own life path unaware of the OL they split off.

"'Each new PL entity becomes an OL within their own dimension having the ability to split their lives to create another PL. All Parallel Lives as well as the Original Lives remember their joined past. However once the split happens each lives their life unaware of the other's life. Each retains and carries forward those people of their past who know them well. Though each entity lives within a completely separate parallel dimension each OL and PL dimension may open to their Others formed from the same OL or each OL may have several PL dimensions which never become aware of their Others.'"

"Whew that's quite a statement," Eliza murmurs then continues to read down the page. "'The PL is the same physically and mentally as the OL at the time of the split until changes encountered or the conditions such as illness or accidents. Each PL becomes an OL letting a PL from it also choose to follow a life path not of the OL.'"

Suddenly Eliza feels as if her head is spinning and she needs fresh air. Leaving the table she goes to the French doors opens them wide and breathes deeply several times. Rubbing her arms she watches the activity on the beach below her house and shivers as she walks back to the book on the table. "Good God did I open Pandora's box when I killed Jack? Is that why these women came to me? Have I created these lives?

Or did one of the other women create me? Who chose what and when? Did they choose another direction when I shot that gun? When did they begin to exist? It didn't really say how or when these Parallel Lives are actually created. All it says is that most are created during childhood. The causes are many: life changes, illness, family breakups, household moves, death of parents or siblings."

Eliza rereads the chapter to the end. When she finishes she looks out the doors at the incoming tide. "Did Jack's life create a life to live in another dimension one good and gentle?" The thought brings a snort of laughter from her and she shakes her head. "Oh no fat chance of that. The SOB would be the same in any life. Wonder where he finally ended up or should I say ended down? No it would have been up as God loves all creatures good and bad. Isn't that what we're taught in church?"

A sudden hunger pang gets her attention and she realizes she hasn't eaten since that quick breakfast in Hood River before she drove back to the beach. Leaving the book open on the table she busies herself with a pan of veggie stir-fry and scampi. The cooking goes quickly and she's soon back at the table eating and rereading the chapter. As she finishes the food she closes the book. "I have to find some sort of activity to focus on besides this or I'm going to be hog-tied and dragged out of here to an asylum."

Taking the dishes to the sink she hand washes and places them in the drainer. Then she wipes the wok before returning it to the hanger over the range. Suddenly thirsty she fills a glass with ice then pours a soda over it. Walking out the French doors she sits on one of the chaise lounges. "Maybe I'll see the women this evening. This time I will talk to them." Leaning back, she soon falls asleep.

The moon hangs overhead when Eliza opens her eyes. She throws her legs off one side of the lounge stands and stretches.

Picking up her glass she goes to the open French door. As she steps inside she sees the two women. Each is exactly as she described them to herself a few hours before. One is sitting on a black leather sofa to her left and the other is sitting directly in front of her on a brown leather sofa. She says nothing as she walks to the right and sits at her own dining table. She leans toward the women so close yet so far.

The women are unaware of her. Studying them Eliza soon realizes the woman on the black leather sofa on the far side of the room is watching the woman on the brown leather sofa in front of the cabin's windows. Eliza suddenly realizes the cabin has no glass or sliders only empty spaces where those should be. As she watches the woman in the cabin walks away from the brown sofa and the woman called Liz turns her head to watch her leave. Soon the woman in the cabin returns to the room with a sleeping bag, blanket, and pillow. She throws the blanket over the sofa then unrolls the bag across it before dropping the pillow on one end. Again she disappears then returns with a flashlight, a can of bug spray and a wool hat on her head.

"Something bad happened to her home or she wouldn't be sleeping out here and not in her bedroom. The windows are gone and everything is soaked. There must have been a hell of a storm. Ah poor thing she must be exhausted and she's zipping herself into the sleeping bag. Just as well she can't hear me."

Watching the woman zip the bag to her chin Eliza is surprised when the sofa and the woman fade from view. "How interesting I can see the woman on the black leather sofa clearer now that the other one is gone. I wonder if she still sees the other one. Maybe she can see me as well as I can see her." Eliza calls to the woman called Liz, "Hello Liz! Can you see me tonight? Now that the other one is gone we should be able to contact each other."

When the woman doesn't seem to hear her Eliza shouts, "I'm over here Liz. I'm Elizabeth Ann Anderson Staples now called Eliza. You said you are Elizabeth Ann Anderson Day and called Liz. Are you of me, or am I of you?" Getting no reaction from the woman Eliza is stymied and sighs. "Damn it what good is seeing these other selves of mine if I can't talk with them?

"Let's see what this book says is the best time for my others to see each other. OK, it says here, 'The best time is a few days before a solstice or equinox. These energies pull apart the connection between all dimensions. This goes on for a few weeks before as well as last for weeks afterward. During these times the universal alignments pull stars, planets, and moons in alignment. Tides are at their highest and lowest and the moon is at its fullest point.'"

Looking at her calendar Eliza tells the woman across the room, "We should be together now. The summer equinox is next week when parallel dimensions open widest to other like dimensions. You and I will get to know each other then, at least I hope so."

CHAPTER THIRTEEN

JUNE 19th

LIZ

LIZ has just reached the edge of the waves and is starting her run to the north cliffs when she hears her name called. Knowing who it is before she turns Liz stiffens with a new fear as she watches Alexandria Petrow exit from the same path through the sand dunes Liz just took. "Bob was right. She's back and she's after me already. Damn," she mutters clenching her fists as Alex runs up the beach. "She must have come back last night. I didn't see her car there yesterday."

For a few seconds Liz's urge to flee almost overwhelms her caution. However she breathes deeply and scolds herself. *Settle down. Alex doesn't know I know. Even if she does we're on the beach and there are too many people. Besides I've been her friend for years. She won't hurt me. At least I hope not.*

Remembering Bob Drake's words of caution she forces a smile as Alex reaches her. "Welcome home Alex. Did you get a lot of work done?"

"Yah go to San Diego. I mean plane to Portland late. We do seminars both places. Yah friend I visit clairvoyant mine teacher. Yah told him of you others. Says Peter return as love you much. Women are parallel lives of you Liz. Same parents same child as you. Trauma event change life from you. Cause other life from yours. You see Liz? You see how he says?"

Liz smiles at Alex's rearranged English. "Are you alright Alex? You sound so agitated. Are you sure you're friend told you the truth? If there're such things as parallel lives why haven't I heard of them before? Does everyone experience these events? Does every dead person return as Peter did? How do you know this man is correct?"

Alex's eyes widen as Liz questions her. "I told you he my teacher. I told you big name of clairvoyants. We see friends. He stays Russia when I go. Now he free come to USA be mine teacher again. Say many died return. Most who see think are crazy. You're a smart girl, Liz. You let you see Peter and others he brought you. Alex sees also. So must be true. You see vat Alex says?"

Liz's smile freezes as Alex struggles to regain the rhythm of the accent she's used for many years. "Yes I see Alex. I see the women every night and I know they are of me or I am of them. They're my parallel lives you say? I didn't know what to call them until now but yes that's exactly what they must be, my parallel lives. Each time I see the women it's as if I'm looking at a video of myself in some other space. We are definitely of each other.

"Last night an astonishing thing happened. I met the woman who loved the black woman who stood in the beam of light with

LIZ

Peter. She's also Elizabeth Ann Anderson but became Beth around the time I became Liz. We met last night in our living rooms. I looked up from my book and there she was looking out her slider doors. From where I sat her cabin was as if Dad had just built it. I spoke to her and she turned and came over to her table which meshes with mine.

"Anyway the woman's name is Beth and she looked right at me. At that moment I knew she saw me as she at first looked frightened then she seemed puzzled. Then she walked over to where our rooms overlap and I stood to greet her. There we were side by side looking at each other just feet apart for some time. Neither of us spoke.

"Finally she reached out and touched me on the face. I did the same. It was wild. Then we held each other still not speaking though we both cried and our hair stood straight up with zaps of static electricity zinging around us. Nothing else happened. We survived. I hugged her and she hugged me back. Words weren't needed. Finally we separated and as we did both rooms meshed together wrapping around us.

"Then Beth told me about her life and I told her about mine. Both our names are Elizabeth Ann Anderson. She goes by Beth. When we sat at our dining tables we moved our chairs close and static electricity snapped around us. It took a few tries before we got the chairs right. It was wonderful Alex. We talked for hours. She and Maxine moved here permanently five years ago when Maxine was diagnosed with terminal colon cancer and wanted her last years to be at Redcliff's. On the uphill side of the cabin they added another bedroom, enlarged the bath, and put locked storage within the open garage, she calls it her carport. I haven't seen that part of her cabin yet. The part I can see is the same cabin Dad built years ago.

"The night Peter came through to me was the same night her Maxine came through to her. Maxine was younger and more beautiful than when they'd first met over thirty years ago. Beth told me about a horrible storm that hit her cabin last week. It trashed everything. Then as if an angel was on her shoulder people came to help and soon the cabin was cleaned out, the windows and glass slider replaced and appliances arrived. By the end of the week the cabin was back to normal and better than before the storm. I'm going to the red cliffs to meet her and slap at our touchstone together. That large round stone in the cliffs that's my touchstone is also hers. We're hoping we'll connect there then we'll try to come back along the beach to our homes together. We feel the more we stay together and connect the more likely we'll be together forever. Peter brought my others to me as a gift from him as an exchange for his dying. Sometimes I feel loosing him was a good thing if I can now have my others with me."

"What say, Liz? How you say that about Peter? Wasn't he your husband for over thirty years? How could anything be worth loss of a beloved husband?"

Shocked by Alex's reaction as well as her English Liz frowns and laughs hollowly. "Oh, Alex, you know very well I didn't mean it that way. Peter's coming back to me brought my others with him and told me to live my new life for myself and my others. This whole thing has given me a new perspective about death and I don't mean just his. He and I talked about so many things after you fled from my house that night.

"Peter told me his plane crash was not an accident and he knew who caused it. He demanded I call Bob Drake who was investigating along with the County Sheriff, FBI, and FAA. They know it was no accident. Peter flew through those mountains many times using instruments. He knew the route with his eyes closed. However a bullet in the engine was something over which he had no control. They are going to make an arrest soon."

"Oh? Yeah? I see. Come, we talk. OK? You visit Alex tell suspicions of crash and tell Peter's truths. Yeah? You not meet

LIZ

Beth you go with Alex." As she speaks Alex grabs onto Liz's arm and begins to pull and twist it as she does.

"Stop that Alex; you're hurting me!" Liz shouts giving Alex a hard shove then rubbing the red marks forming on her forearm. Her heart races as she hadn't anticipated Alex's reaction to Bob's words would be so profound. "I'm going to see Beth by myself at the red rocks. I can't stop you from running on the beach just not with me. Don't even try. Now I'm going to meet Beth."

Seeing the look on Liz's face Alex steps back though she barks, "You stay, Liz! Summer solstice is tomorrow. Universal dimensions pull apart. Someone in other dimension they get lost in dimension forever. I go meet Beth. Alex will keep you safe."

Shaking with anger Liz hisses at Alex as she sidesteps the woman, "I said you aren't coming with me. Do you hear me? Leave me alone. Go home and fix that stupid accent you seem to have lost."

The look on Alex's face tells Liz she has said way too much.

CHAPTER FOURTEEN

JUNE 19th

BETH and LIZ

LIZ slows to a walk as she nears the slab of red stone at the base of the cliffs. Feeling a tingle run over her arms she breathes deeply refusing to look back to see if Alex has followed. When she climbs onto the slab of stone the air around her thickens and the light turns a deep gold. "Beth where are you? It's me Liz. I'm at our touchstone at the red cliffs. You are of me Beth and I am of you."

As she speaks the dense air wraps around her and her hair rises up snapping wildly over her head as though in a field of static electricity. Long sparks dance over her short white hair causing it to shimmer like a halo. When Liz turns back to the beach to see if Alex followed her she sees only the golden fog she stands within. Then the glow brightens and Liz feels another presence on the red rock. "Beth? You must be close as I'm putting on quite a show with static electricity. Where are you? Get on the red stone. Let's hit our touchstone together. Beth?"

Suddenly a multicolored shape moves to her left elbow and bumps into her. Liz gasps. "Beth is that you? Damn it Beth where are you?"

"It's me Liz I'm here." Beth laughs grabbing Liz's hand. "I'm here. We've made it here together. Who'd ever believe us? Parallel lives you and me side by side in broad daylight. Let's hit our touchstone together. Ready? I declare this run good and done!" both shout as they slap the large protruding red stone embedded in the cliff's vertical wall.

Beth holds Liz at arms length to look directly into her eyes. Tears wet their cheeks as they look at each other. Seeing their white hair whip above each head as brilliant sparks of static electricity brings whoops of laughter from each woman. Holding tight to each other's hands both women study the mirrored face before them. Each face has the same arched brows, blue eyes, freckles across a short nose with full lips pulled into a wide smile, a smile so wide each looks a bit clownish. Beth laughs. "Holy cow, Liz we have the same freckles and all. I guess there's no denying we're of each other. This must be what identical twins feel like. Lucky my hair is longer or I wouldn't know which one I am."

"Oh, Beth, you're so right. We're too much, aren't we? Look how exact we are. The freckles on our arms are in the same spots. Do you have a birthmark on your knee? Yup just like mine. Have you seen the other one like us whose house is larger than both in our homes' dimensions? She's a bit heavier and her hair is different but she still looks like both of us. Have you seen her?"

"I think I saw her before Maxine died and about once a week since. We'll have to watch for her tonight at the tables. For now though let's finish our talk. We stopped when our childhoods separated, didn't we? We shared the first fourteen years of our lives until the accident that killed your parents and sister and changed my Dana forever. That must be when one of us split from the other when we became two entities as one Elizabeth split into two."

Liz nodded. "We know we were both in the accident. I was terribly injured and didn't know the rest of my family had died until months afterward. When I was finally able to be moved I went to live with my Aunt Maggie Mom's older sister. She was wonderful. She was a widow. Her husband Lee had been killed in WWII. Maggie loved me as a daughter. I was so lucky to have her. We came to Dad's cabin every summer and holiday.

"After high school graduation I went to the University of Washington in Seattle where I met Peter. He was finishing his doctorate." Liz smiles at the memory. "It was love at first sight for me. Later he said it was for him too but he was too deep into his research to notice any woman or do anything about it if he did. Aunt Maggie was a favorite of his. She passed away five years ago. I still miss her very much."

Beth nods. "Your accident sounds horrible. Ours was more of a fender bender. Dana refused to wear a seat belt and flew past Mom and into the windshield. Before that Dana had been a warm kind person. Afterward she turned horrid to the whole family. The neurologist said head injuries often cause a personality to flip-flop. Dad felt guilty about what happened until the day he died. Dana used his feelings against him and Mom to get at me even though they sent her to see many doctors nothing helped.

"Things got really horrible when I brought Maxine home to meet my folks. They loved her immediately and made Maxine their third daughter. Dana had married one of her doctors, Ed Gowan and they were on an extended honeymoon. When they got back Mom held a family picnic to introduce Max to the rest of the family and Dana and Ed. At first it was great seeing them however by mid-afternoon Dana began talking about how was it possible that Maxine chose me and not her. Yes you heard me right. Dana had not met Max before that day yet she had a screaming fit about why anyone would chose me over her. Even when Maxine and I explained that we were lesbians she kept shouting at us. Finally Ed had enough of her display and literally yanked her into their car and took her home."

"Though your Dana sounds horrid you did have your parents for many more years. Aunt Maggie was so wonderful to me but I still miss my folks and sister so much. What did your parents say when you told them you are a lesbian?"

Beth laughed. "They were wonderful. They worried about our safety as others back then people were so manic about mixed races and god forbid being lesbian. Gay was still another word for joy which of course is why we gays began to use it. It was lovely to have the folks with us for as many years as we did. A few days after Max and I said our vows to each other Dad was killed by a mugger while walking his dog Amber. The asshole even shot poor Amber when she tried to protect Dad. It was so stupid. Dad never carried money only a well-used credit card and a few dollars.

"When Mom became ill she offered the cabin to both Dana and Max and me. Dana said she didn't want anything to do with that piece of crap of a cabin or the queers who would share it with her. She wanted money. I got the cabin appraised then found money to buy Dana out completely. The papers she signed eliminated any claim she had on the cabin or the land adjoining it. By then even Aunt Margret had turned away from Dana.

"Liz I just realized your Aunt Maggie must be my mom's sister Margaret and you are right she was a darling. She passed away a couple years after Mom did. She and Mom were very close and both loved Max. When the three of them were together they'd play Cribbage nonstop." Beth glowed as she told of their work at the University and the beach house. Finally Beth says, "Enough of me now let's hear about you."

Liz squeezes Beth's hands. "I love hearing about your life. I wish I had more to tell you about mine. I told you most of it last night. I'm a writer. Do travel articles for a magazine and am working on a couple books. Mostly this week I've thought about little else than the three of us. Do you realize that both Peter and Maxine died on June 1 at two in the afternoon? Think of that. Did their deaths on that date cause our dimensions to open to each other?

"What about the other of us? Did she lose her man at the same time? Will we be together for months or years? Have you thought of what you'll do now that you're without Maxine? I think of little else. How will I fill my hours, days, weeks, years without Peter? Now that I know you exist I want you here with me always. We must make it happen somehow any way we can even if it's only within our cabins or at our touchstone here at the red cliffs."

Seeing the worry in Liz's eyes Beth nods. "I agree. Meeting you last night was so phenomenal. I couldn't get to sleep from thinking of who you are, who we are. I thought losing Maxine was the worst I would have to endure yet I've come to realize that losing you would be almost as devastating. Knowing you existed beyond my dimension and not ever seeing you again is too frightening for me to put my mind around. I was blessed to have Maxine for over thirty wonderful years. I am blessed to have you for these two days. Oh God Liz we must we must stay together within our joined dimensions. We must."

Suddenly Beth begins to sob as she wraps her arms around Liz who holds her gently and pats her back whispering words of assurance. Finally Beth pulls a frayed tissue from her pocket wipes her face and blows her nose. "Man oh man did I ever need that cry. It's been tough having to keep the stiff upper lip all the time. I'm the sort who needs direction. Max gave me that. I need projects with purpose. I had a lot to do after the storm. Now the cabin's better than ever and I'm on very shaky ground right now. I sent Max's things off to whoever could best use them. We both believed that letting go allows others into your life. I don't want to lose you or the other you must stay with me. We need to learn about each of our worlds and be together for years to come."

Liz agrees. "Peter's only been gone for three weeks yet his presence is everywhere. I'm alive. Still there seems to be only a small part of me in my own home. I know what I'm saying sounds selfish Beth but I want the house to be mine. Half the time I hate him for leaving me and the other half I'm mourning his being gone. A week ago his partner Bob Drake came over and we emptied Peter's office. Let me tell you what I found out about my darling Peter and our neighbor Alex. Spies have been in Redcliff's all the while I've lived here. It's amazing and I feel as if I've lived in a James Bond movie. Let's walk back together and I'll tell you all about it and the money I found."

As they step off the slab of red rock the golden fog wraps around them letting them walk within their meshed dimensions chattering like old friends ignoring their hair snaps and flashes overhead. They enjoy the beach and stop whenever they come upon a shell or unusual pebble or hunk of driftwood. Whatever it is they look it over carefully and one or the other decides to carry it to their home or they agree to toss it back to the ocean. However they never let go of their other's hand.

When they near their homes the golden fog opens to show them they are in front of the path to both their homes. Liz turns to Beth and sees that she is standing beside a newly dozed sand dune. Each sees her own home as the fog slowly clears.

Both feel an increasing tingle down their arms into their joined hands.

As Liz finishes her story she tells Beth, "There are so many wonderful causes I can use that money for and nobody will know. All those years Peter and Alexandria were spies working against each other and I was so naïve. No, I was damned stupid. Now I know to be frightened of Alex. How could I have believed her story of being a defected Soviet ballerina? I shudder at how my chatter about Peter aided her work against him or this country. The only time I pushed her away was after Peter's death. She kept demanding she should help me go through his things. Then after I scattered Peter's ashes at the cliffs I came home to find her trying to force the lock on Peter's office door. Even then she was so cool and simply said she needed the books she'd loaned Peter. I told her the keys to the door went down in the plane with him. At the time I really thought that as I'd forgotten where Peter hid the spares. She left very angry that I wouldn't talk to her as I'd done before. My heart wasn't ready for her or anyone else. I needed to be alone and told her to go away.

"Late last night Bob called to tell me Alex would be in Redcliff's today. She is. I saw her on the beach today when I was coming to meet you. She scared me. I'll see her tonight I'm certain of it. I wasn't supposed to say anything except what Bob had told me to. I did though. I told her to go home and fix her broken accent. All these years I thought she was my very good friend and all the while she was Peter's nemesis."

CHAPTER FIFTEEN

JUNE 19th

ELIZA

ELIZA realizes her morning runs to the cliffs are faster each day. *It's so great to be able to run like this again. I don't feel the pain anymore as my thoughts are focused on the two women in my front room. They come every day and night yet they don't see me. At times they are so close I try to touch them when we are sitting at our dining tables. When I do they disappear for several minutes before they come back within my home. They're exactly like me and have to be some sort of part of me. Though they came right after Jack's death I no longer think they are here because I killed him and I know I'm not crazy or seeing hallucinations. I think his death opened my dimension to theirs. I wonder if they each lost a loved one. I need to talk to them. I remember that the woman Liz said she had lost her husband. It's so frustrating that they aren't seeing me anymore. I wish I'd stayed with them when they asked me to stay. Now I don't know if I'll ever talk with them. The two seem so animated when they're together at the tables each night. They were there* *again this morning. I tried to touch them and that caused them to disappear. Sure they always come back but they don't see me. Well tomorrow's the solstice. My book on metaphysics says the connections between parallel lives are strongest during the hours before during or after each solstice. If I don't meet them today or tomorrow I may never have a chance again. I may never have a connection with them. I'll sit all night talking to them even if they don't see or hear me. I will invite them into my life."*

As Eliza turns off the beach onto the path through the dunes to her home, she slows and thinks of her achievement. *I've dropped ten pounds. Now Dana and I can race to our touchstone when she moves here at the end of the month. I'm so glad I remodeled the house to include rooms for her. She loves Redcliff's as much as I do. It wasn't her fault that her money was needed for treatments for Jim. I have more than enough for both of us. Besides when she sells her home, she'll have her own money again.*

From the top step to the deck she sees a large heavy man lying in one of the chaise lounges on the south side of the deck. He is sound asleep with his head flopped to the far side. Frowning at the huge stomach rising and falling as he breathes she recognizes Mike Hartman. Still she hollers at him from the top step, "Hey you! What the hell are you doing sleeping here on my deck lounge? What do you want?"

Startled the man struggles upright looking dazed and embarrassed. "Eliza? It's Mike. Mike Hartman. Sorry if I scared you. I fell asleep. Came here because I need you to answer questions about Peg and Jack, you have time?"

"Sure Mike. I have questions for you too. Wait right there and I'll get us some iced tea and brownies. We'll sit over there at the table. It's too nice to be inside." Eliza smiles as she talks to him then waves to her closest neighbors to the south when they turn to watch. Al and Penny never miss a thing along the full three miles of 'their beach'. The couple wave back then return to their books and newspapers.

In her kitchen, Eliza's smile fades as she reminds herself *I know nothing, nothing. Not one thing. I know nothing of Peg or Jack. I know nothing. I know nothing at all. Do you Mike? Did you do it? Did you?*

The last thought brings the smile back to Eliza's face as she carries their refreshments to the table on the deck. "Over here Mike. It'll be easier to talk face to face at the table. Have a brownie. No breakfast this morning, and I'm starved."

"Can I help?" Mike asks as his heavy body lunges off the lounge and thuds across the deck to the table.

Sitting in the shaded area under the eaves Eliza stuffs a brownie into her mouth as she shakes her head. "Take a brownie fresh last night. Need a napkin?"

For several minutes neither speaks as they eat brownies and drink cold tea. Finally all the food is gone and they both speak at the same time.

"So, how did you…"

"I want to know…"

Each stops and looks at the other waiting for the awkward moment to pass.

Eliza flicks a hand toward Mike. "You go first."

"Sorry to come here but I need to know if you knew anything about Jack and Peg's affair before you left Hood River. Did you?"

"Good Lord no. Never thought it and would never have imagined it. Not because of Jack though good Lord no but because Peg professed to hate him so much. Hated him for treating me the way he did. She spoke harshly about his affairs. The last time I saw her was the day before I left Hood River she came over to say goodbye and while we talked she told me what an ass Jack had been to a friend of hers." Eliza shakes her head and a sad bewildered look crosses her face. "It was a shock when Frank told me what happened. It's still unbelievable. Neither one of them deserved to die that way. Even Jack the poor asshole didn't deserve to die that way. It's too terrible for words."

She saw the question in his eye. "No Mike I didn't kill them. Nor could I have done so. I was here with witnesses all around who saw me all that day here and in town. Everyone may think it but it never happened. I hated what he did to our life. I was done with both him and Hood River when I moved here. Even with the mansion which I've now turned over to the school district for special events and classes. I've set up a trust for its upkeep.

"Everyone always wondered why I stayed with Jack. That is so obvious I'm surprised anyone ever questioned it. As I told the grand jury I stayed for my mother-in-law Minna after she made me heir to the Staples fortune. The power she gave me with that generous gesture was worth all of Jacks shit. I would have left years ago if she had not told me her plan or given me a copy of her will to hold. I thanked her profusely for having such faith in my judgment and business abilities. Was I hurt by what Jack did over the years? Hell yes. Though the first ten years were wonderful the rest are best forgotten. Then Minna made her decision and it was easy after that. Power makes many things look very different.

"At the reading of Minna's will Jack was furious when he heard he did not inherit the fortune. He threatened to kill me in front of everyone in the lawyer's office. I was so frightened I stayed in that office with the lawyers until everything was transferred to my name. If I die my estate goes to my family and to charities Minna cared about. She was wonderful to me. It's been a great life. I loved being the grand dame of the Staples Mansion and Fruit Packing business and I won't deny that I loved holding it over Jack. I wouldn't change a thing. Being married to Jack was interesting to say the least as there was never a dull moment. It's given me great material for a book which I'm going to write."

As she speaks she sees Mike study her face and her gestures. He touches the front of his shirt several times and taps his fingers on one of the buttons. Eliza laughs. "Why Mike Hartman I do believe you think I killed Jack and Peg. That is so funny. All this past week I believed it was you. Peg knew the entry code to the mansion as my trusted friend. She kept the code in her address book by the kitchen phone where you could find it any time.

"Why didn't I tell the sheriff that fact you ask? Guess I figured if that stupid bastard of a sheriff was a friend of yours and Jack's all these years he was too stupid to figure that out. The good old boys' club is alive and thriving in Hood River. You must have known about Peg and Jack. Why else did you take up with your woman in New York City? Yes you knew about Peg's affair. I see it in your eyes. You killed them didn't you Mike?"

Shaking his head frantically Mike's eyes bulge from their sockets as veins pulse along his forehead, "No." he screamed. "No damn you. I was in Chili for two weeks then in New York City when they were killed. Frank checked it out. I loved Peg. I loved Jack. He was my good friend."

"Yes wasn't he? And Peg was your good wife. It must be a terrible thing to be cuckolded by your wife who screwed your friend. Now it's known by everyone. That must make it a thousand times worse. Yeah you did it Mike. You knew about them.

Come on confess to me. Nobody will ever know. Congratulations on doing it so cleanly. I've spent many an hour trying to reconstruct how you did it. Where's the gun? Was it the one she found in a pawnshop on that trip to Denver? Wasn't it an antique pistol from a real gunslinger? Yes that's what it was I remember now. I'm right aren't I? Mike?"

Mike stood so fast he overturned the heavy deck chair where he sat. "Damn you damn you!" he screamed. "I said I didn't have a thing to do with their deaths. Damn you, you bitch. Why would you say those things? I loved Peg. Sure I had a fling with that woman but I loved Peg. I never wanted a divorce. I wouldn't hurt her for nothing. She was my darling my dear friend. She was my soul."

Shouting and shaking his fists at her Mike pulls at his shirt front loosening a bunch of wires taped to his chest. Three buttons pop open in his effort exposing the wires taped to a shaved patch of his hairy chest. "Damn you! Now they think I did it you bitch! You confess or I'll kill you too. Do you hear me? I'll kill you too!"

As Mike lunges across the table at her Eliza throws herself sideways onto the deck and screams, "Help! Help! Mike's killing me!"

In his fury Mike pushes the table over trying to grab Eliza's arm. She swiftly rolls to one side wrapping her legs around Mike's. In that moment she pulls him off balance causing him to fall with a thud onto the deck next to her. Untangling her legs Eliza stands against the railing and screams at the couple sitting on the deck about fifty feet to the south. "Help me; help me! Al, Penny. Help me! Call nine-one-one. Mike Hartman is attacking me! He killed Jack and now he's trying to kill me!"

At first the couple watched the activity on Eliza's deck with great curiosity. When she screams waves her arms and shouts

ELIZA

for help they spring into action. Al races down their steps to the trail through the dunes while Penny picks up her phone and dials. Seeing their quick response Eliza chuckles. *There is no better watchdog than a nosy neighbor. Thank you, Al and Penny.*

Still kicking at Mike she sees a wad of wires lying near him. Scooping them up Eliza shouts into them, "You can't hurt me Mike! My neighbors are coming. The police will get you for killing Peg and Jack after all! Murderer! Give up murderer!"

Struggling to get his awkward body onto his feet Mike staggers past Eliza swinging his fists at her and shouting, "Damn you. Eliza I'll kill you too!" Though he misses her she falls onto the deck. Then he turns down the north side deck to the driveway. Eliza smiles at the wires in her hands and whispers into them, "He's running away now. But he was going to use these wires to strangle me. That's must be why he hid them in his shirt. Thank God he's so out of shape. I'll give these to the police when they get here."

Scrambling to her feet Eliza follows him to the driveway where she points at his car roaring south on Shoreline Drive. "Stop him he's a murderer!"

When Al reaches her Eliza is truly sobbing with relief. "Who was that guy?" he asks panting to catch his breath. "Was that who killed Jack?" He starts to put an arm around Eliza then pulls it away as Penny rushes down the driveway to where they stand.

"I called the sheriff. They'll get him. There is only one road out of this end of the beach. Did we hear right? Is he the man who killed Jack and that woman in your home in Hood River?"

"Yes, yes. It was Mike Hartman. He killed Jack and his wife Peg. He came to kill me! At first he said he wanted to talk. I thought he was a friend. Then he attacked me. He had this bunch of wires and tried to strangle me with them. He kept saying he would kill me too. When he said that I knew he was the killer. Thank you both so much for coming to help me. I don't know what I'd have done if you and Al hadn't been outside today Penny! Thanks so much for calling the sheriff. It's so good to have wonderful neighbors like you and Al. Thank you so much."

"You should also know that man was here most of the time you were on your run," Penny said. "We saw him drive down the driveway and then he was on the deck. He disappeared into your house for several minutes maybe fifteen. Al had just stood to go check on him when he came out to the deck. When he saw us he waved hello with a big smile. We figured he was a friend of yours so we waved back. Soon he lay down on the lounge and fell asleep. As I said he must have been in the house for at least fifteen minutes. Maybe you should check to see if you're missing anything."

"Thank you I'll do that. Thanks so much. I think I'll lie down until the sheriff gets here."

Along the side deck she picks up some of the wires she'd dropped and studies them for several minutes. Again she smiles. *I'll be damned these wires have transmitters on them. Mike was bugged. I wonder who put him up to that. Frank Gilbert? Could he be that stupid? What did he think I would say? I'm shocked that he would do such a thing. I'll give this mess to the local sheriff when he comes.*

Later after the deputy sheriff takes her statement and leaves with the wires Eliza remembers Penny saying that Mike had been inside her home for several minutes. That could only mean one thing. Going to her kitchen phone she unscrews the mouthpiece tips it over her palm and is not surprised when a small black plastic chip falls into it. Placing it in a small dish she then goes from room to room finding several more in other phones and stuck under counters and shelves. Now she knows she must not talk to herself until all the bugs are found. For the next hour she hunts for them in every room. Finally when she has nearly a dozen in the dish she takes them out to the water's edge and flips them into the waves.

Back inside her house she decides to call Sheriff Frank Gilbert. "I need to talk to the Sheriff Frank Gilbert. What? Where is he? When he comes back tell him Eliza Staples called. Tell him to call me ASAP. I must talk to him today right away. Let him know that Mike Hartman was here and tried to kill me. The local deputy was here and took my statement."

Two minutes after she hangs up the phone it rings. Picking up the receiver Eliza is surprised to hear Frank Gilbert's voice. "Frank? Mike Hartman was here and attacked me. He tried to kill me! Yes he did. Yes! He knocked me down kicked at me and then swung to knock me out. If it weren't for my brave neighbors, he would have finished me. He's your murderer. Said so himself. Yes Frank, Mike told me he would kill me too. *Too*, Frank. Do you realize what that means? He killed Peg and Jack and will kill me too. Yes I'm inside with my doors and windows locked. My neighbors are watching my house from their deck. They saw him attack me. Yes Frank it was terrifying! There's no telling what he'll try next. You take care too Frank."

As Eliza hangs up the phone she smiles. "Of course it all makes sense. Mike killed Jack and Peg on the first of June. Who else could it be?"

CHAPTER SIXTEEN

JUNE 19th

TOGETHER

LIZ doesn't feel Beth's hand leave hers. It simply evaporates as she walks toward her home. Realizing they are both again within their own dimensions she runs inside to sit at her dining table. When Beth doesn't appear at once she hurries to use the bathroom then grabs a can of soda from the fridge. She pops it open as she sits down at her dining table. The can is half full when Beth appears across their tables from her. "Hi Liz, sorry I'm late I had to use the bathroom."

Liz laughs. "I did too. What a morning we've had. I'll never forget how our hair zapped and flashed when we slapped our touchstone together and the walk back was just as wild. It was amazing. I realize now how different your beach is from mine. Tell me about it and Dad's cabin. Are there any cabins or resorts nearby? Or is it the same as when we were kids?"

"Neither, so many things have happened. The cabins and other buildings were swept from the beach by a horrific storm right after Dad died. The cabin made it through because of the high dunes below it and the fact it sits on this high point of rock. Now it's the only cabin left on the seven-mile strip of Redcliff's Beach. A couple months ago I signed the cabin and land over to the State of Washington for a preserve to be named in Maxine's honor. When I die the beach will be kept as a preserve. Max and I wanted to give the Pacific Ocean a break and this stretch of beach is to be used for oceanography research and life resources to enrich those to the seas north and south of us.

"The cabin is the same in this area where we are now. However, when we moved here Maxine and I added a guest room and enlarged the bathroom thus enclosing the carport. Now the front door goes into the carport. We planned to add a garage door but found we enjoyed it open. I may use a bit of the insurance money from the storm damage to get a door added. I was very lucky this time.

"That storm tore away the last of the sand dunes. All those wonderful high dunes of our childhood are gone. The wharf-builder has worked wonders pushing mounds of sand around pilings he's sunk into the sand. The cabin is quite protected again and he's moving more sand into dunes up toward the cliffs. There was nothing between the ocean and the cabin when he started now there is a grand row of man-made dunes. I don't think the State would like the changes however I don't care. That dear man has done miracles doing whatever he could to hold tides and storms back for another decade or two. Do you have any storm damage?"

"No. Peter and I were very lucky. We had a lot of winds though no real storms. When I first saw you in your cabin you were getting ready to sleep on the sofa in the main room. The cabin looked wet and well scrubbed. Now it looks normal. You were so lucky to have gotten help right away."

"Yes," Beth agreed, smiling softly. "I feel as if an angel named Maxine must have sat on my shoulder all the while. Those crews my insurance man sent did magic getting the place emptied and washed out. George Ames sent an electrician to rewire everything the second day when the new windows, slider doors were set in the spaces. Finally a big truck came with all the new appliances I'd ordered from Sears. In fact the cabin's better than ever thanks to the crew and getting the dunes and bulkheads back to normal. Tom Ames is still working north of the cabin on dunes near the cliffs. Yesterday he brought pallets of sea grass starts for each of the new dunes and I spent the day poking them into the dunes. I've got most of those nearest the cabin topped though I still have about five more to do up north. And yes, I'm footing the bill for everything. I sure hope he's right about those dunes holding back the storms or I'll have no choice next time but to move out."

"Enjoy the days you have here Beth. You're lucky to have the beach so much to yourself. It must be wonderful. My Redcliff's Beach is a small town and Dad's stand of woods above the cabin is the last undeveloped piece along the beachside strip. I've been offered mega bucks for it but I can't sell. My Dana wanted to build her cabin up there. So I feel as if it's a memorial to her and our folks. This beach still has high wide dunes. In fact they spread a thousand feet out to the highest tide. What happened to your woods?"

"Those storms blew the trees down even before they took out the cabins. We cut them up for fire wood before we changed to propane It's nothing but sand all around here now. My Dana goes crazy when she sees me still living in the cabin she didn't want. I've had to get an injunction to keep her away from here. Several months before Maxine died Dana came to the cabin when I was in town and chased Max into the bathroom. When I came home I found Dana pounding on the door and threatening her. I threw a chair at Dana then ran for my shotgun. I would have killed that damned woman if she hadn't moved so fast. I did shoot the back windows of her car to smithereens. A couple hours later her husband Ed called for an explanation. When I told him what Dana had done to Maxine he exploded. I don't want to know what happened. I just know Dana didn't show up for several months not until last week. I may have to get a large dog just to warn me when she comes around and to keep my sanity." Beth laughs trying to keep things light.

"Peter and I talked about getting a dog many times," Liz says a bit wistfully. "A dog to run with me to the cliffs would be great. It would also be good protection to have around with the way things are with Alex. She really scared me this morning when she grabbed my arm and twisted it. Good thing the beach was so full of people. She couldn't hurt me without giving herself away. I'm telling you Beth if I find out she's connected to Peter's death in any way I will kill her somehow. That money I found makes almost anything possible." Liz laughed, "You do realize, Beth, I would never say these things to anyone else?"

"Oh yes I realize that and tell you that five years ago the man who killed my dad was released from prison and I followed him home and shot him, simple as that. They didn't investigate very long and I was never questioned. It gave me great joy to have gotten rid of such a rotten person for the rest of the human race. I think more victims should to do the same."

CHAPTER SEVENTEEN

JUNE 19th

ELIZA

ELIZA knows she can not live comfortably if there is a chance there are any of Mike's bugs left stuck around in her home. So she jumps into Charlie and heads for the Mall in Aberdeen to see if there is some sort of electronic device to find them. *Someone at the electronics store will know what I need. I'll be a woman distressed by an ugly divorce and a vicious husband. That sounds almost real.* She smiles as she pulls into a parking spot right in front of the door.

The only clerk is young. *My God he looks no more than twelve years old. What can he possibly know about anything?* Even with the thought still in her head Eliza smiles shyly as she approaches the young man. Clearing her throat she nods to him when he looks at her.

"Hello. May I interrupt you for a few minutes? I'm hoping you can give me some advice. The thing is I think my house has been bugged by my ex-husband. We're going through a rather messy divorce right now and he's determined to find something against me. He won't admit I'm innocent and he's the one who's had a dozen affairs. The problem is I've found a few small round black plastics things under my counters and tables and a friend told me they were bugs to listen to what is going on around them. I've found eight and think there may be more. Is there something I can buy to find these things easier?"

The young man waits until she finishes her explanation before nodding very seriously. "There's an easy fix for that. Do you have an old-style cell phone?"

Without speaking Eliza shows him her new BlackBerry.

"Nope that won't do, too new and won't pick up interference. You need an old-style cell phone. Follow me." They walk through the store and he picks up a small display phone off the shelf and turns it on and hands it to Eliza. "Here's the kind you need."

Eliza takes the phone from him and holds it to her ear. "What should I hear?"

"Walk to those lamps over there. Hold it close." She does as instructed. "Hear that buzz? That's electronic interference. You just make calls then walk around your house. When you hear that buzz you know other electronic equipment is nearby. Those things you're looking for are microchips that send messages. Not much call for this phone anymore. Just sell it to old people. That's the last one. You can have it for ten bucks and I'll program it for you."

After the young man sets up the cell phone with the company of Eliza's choice she pops it into her purse and digs out the money. "Will that twenty cover the taxes and your help? Thanks."

Summer traffic is out in full force when she leaves the store making it a slow drive back to the beach house. Taking the phone from her purse she calls her sister in Hood River to chat. The phone is still ringing when it emits a loud buzz. Moving it slowly across the car's dashboard she finds a bug behind the rearview mirror.

"Damn. Here's another one of those things. Mike must have planted it here. I wonder what the hell he thought he was going to hear. I don't have anything to hide," she shouts into the bug before dropping it out the car window. As she drives down to the front of her garage she dials Staples Fruit Packing Company and asks for the new CEO who replaced Jack after he died knowing she will get a long-winded update from the arrogant man. He does as she expects and for the next half hour she goes over both cars and the house finding four more bugs. Finally Eliza is sure the place is clean and the CEO is becoming repetitive so she tells him, "I've got to go now. Thanks for the update. It sounds as if Staples is doing great under your management. Congratulations on your good work."

Again Eliza goes out to the beach and throws the chips into the ocean. When she returns she passes the deck table and benches and stops. *Mike was out here for some time before I got back from my run.* Again dialing the Staples number she moves the phone over the top of the table and benches. She finds two bugs under the edge of the large dish of sedums in the center of the table but the table and benches are clean. Laughing about her misdial to Staples' receptionist she wanders back to the waves. "I declare this job good and done," she tells the devises in her hand as she drops them into the water.

CHAPTER EIGHTEEN

JUNE 19th

LIZ

LIZ empties the contents of the large manila envelope Bob Drake left her onto the dining table. It's filled with photos of Alexandria Petrow in various cities or countries around the world. There are over fifty photos all taken without Alex's awareness. Some are close up while others were taken from far distances and are rather fuzzy. There are also several passports Alex's photo with other names.

Anxious and more than a little frightened Liz goes to the pantry to get the brownie mix and whips up a double batch of the dark chocolate mix. While she waits for the oven timer to go off Liz goes outside to the deck railing to watch the last streaks of sunset. Brilliant reds flick across the tops of the waves then kisses the sand dunes to a blushing pink with purple shadows. Her thoughts are of loving Peter all those years and never really knowing who he was. Turning to look over the dunes to Alex's house Liz wonders if the phone calls she'll make will bring Alex over or will this old friend now enemy flee Redcliff's for good. A sudden chill crosses her shoulders causing Liz to hug herself. At the same moment the timer goes off and she hurries to check the brownies. The house is filled with the aroma of melting chocolate and she pulls insulated mitts from a drawer to open the oven door and poke a knife into the center of the hot cake. When the knife comes out clean she lifts the hot dish onto a cooling rack.

Looking at the clock she sees it is time for the first call to Alexandria. Liz picks up the receiver and quickly dials Alex's number. As the phone rings someone nearby, shouts, "Oh that smells yummy!" Startled Liz drops the phone back into its cradle and shouts, "Beth is that you?" Though no one answers Liz hurries to her dining table and sits on the chair she uses when talking with Beth.

At that moment the mantle clock chimes eight. Realizing she must call Alex.. When the voice mail picks up Liz repeats the words Bob Drake told her to say. "Hey Alex I just baked a batch of brownies. Come over and have a couple and let's talk. I have an envelope I kept from Peter's office as it's filled with photos of you and I thought you'd like to have them. If you don't want them just call and I'll dump them in the garbage. Let me know one way or the other?"

After that she goes first to the slider to make certain it is unlocked then she goes into Peter's office to call Bob Drake. When he answers she tells him, "I called Alex and left the message. Her house is dark and I'm beginning to doubt that she's home."

"She's home and she heard your message. Stay put. Don't call again. She'll be there soon so don't panic. Do what I told you to do. Go behind your kitchen counter and stay there no matter what. When she confronts you with a gun, drop to the floor and roll to the far side of the kitchen. No ad-libbing this time Liz. Say your lines and drop. You hear me?"

"Yes I hear you. Be on time that's all I ask." Not saying goodbye Liz drops the phone and hurries back to the kitchen. The brownies are cool enough to cut so she slips them out to a large platter and puts the baking dish in the sink running water into it. A rush of sadness sweeps over her. Her life has changed so quickly this past month. She's lost her husband then met one of her two others and now a former friend is going to kill her. "Or at least try to kill me. I must remember Bob's directions and don't' wait too long and give her a chance to take aim."

Standing at the kitchen sink, Liz looks out the kitchen window at the south beach musing on what her future may bring, "Letting go of Alex is easy if I can have Beth and Eliza with me. Tomorrow's the solstice. Our dimensions have to tie together or push further apart. Please let me stay linked to them forever even if it's only at our joined dining tables. I need these ladies in my life."

Suddenly a soft breeze brushes her cheek causing Liz to look toward the slider door. It is now fully open and a woman dressed totally in a black hooded sweatshirt and tights walks through it into the room. She moves silently as if Liz is not there crossing the room to stand beside the dining table. Very slowly the woman picks up each photo and passport to study them very carefully.

To Liz the scene is too weird and she suddenly laughs loudly. "Good God Alex you look amazingly like a character out of an old Hitchcock movie. Are you going to a costume party as a cat burglar?" Smiling broadly she continues. "What was the name of that film? You know the one where Cary Grant is a jewel thief and Grace Kelly falls for him?"

Without answering Alex sets down the passports she had been studying and said. "We do have a nice little collection here. You do this? Ah, no, I see it was Peter." Turning directly to Liz she shakes her head with a sneer. "Elizabeth Ann Anderson alias Liz

Day we seem to have a hit a big snag in our relationship. What should be done about it? Huh? Cat burglar got your tongue?" Alex laughs as she pulls a pistol with a long silencer attached to the front end of the barrel from a holster under her left arm.

Liz gasps at the sudden reality of the moment and can only watch the pistol in wide-eyed wonder. Alex waves the gun watching Liz's eyes follow the movement. "Tell me my friend, you prepared for my version of how to end this storybook tale of you and Peter being so in love? Or do you have plans to write your own ending?"

Liz laughs as she repeats the words Bob Drake gave her to say: "Why Alex what ever happened to your accent? Your English is perfect. Peter was right all along wasn't he? He always said no ever-so-proud Russian ballerina would speak the bastardized English you did for so many years. He wondered how you got so cleanly away during the sixties when all the others who escaped Russia had to hide or be dragged back kicking and screaming. Then the Soviet Union broke apart and you hardly blinked an eye nor shed nary a tear. Not even a vodka toast to the new Republic. Who pays you for your fine lifestyle? Are you really that good a clairvoyant?"

Liz knows she has said too much and it's way past time to duck under the counter when Alex suddenly sits down at the table and sets the gun on the pile of photos. "Aw that is your biggest problem Liz your mind is too curious. You always had too many questions. Where'd I been with whom and why did I go? Oh my you prattled on and on. Let me tell you I work for many and any if the price is right the deed is done. However I digress. The problem is what to do about you. Got any ideas? You've been such a faithful little friend for so long and an excellent informer so to speak. I delighted in our friendship and it breaks my heart that it must end. You are the only person I allowed to come close to me all these years. My family was long gone and bastards anyway. As for old Soviet friends they are business partners and one should never get close to business partners. Don't you agree?

"Therefore my dear Elizabeth Anderson I can not have you walking around talking to one and all nor can I leave this evidence in your keeping. These passports I lost somewhere on one of my Austrian trips. I saw Peter over there though it never dawned on me that he was clever enough to be anything more than a bean counter. So my dear friend this is too bad for you and very bad for me as I loved living at Redcliff's. You were so sweet and gullible and eager to believe everything I told you about my clients. That by the way it is true that I am clairvoyant and I do have many rich and famous clients who use my services in several different ways."

As Alex grabs the pistol to take aim, Liz drops to the floor and shouts, "If you're so clairvoyant Alex you must know there are agents all around you and you should lay down your gun if you want to live!" Rolling until she hits the pantry door alcove she lies flat along the base.

At the moment she dropped to the floor two soft pops can be heard and two tiles behind the kitchen sink shatter. Realizing they would have killed her if she had not dropped so quickly Liz is too stunned to move further and lays still as a stone her breaths soft and shallow. Suddenly two loud shots come from a gun without a silencer causing Liz's ears to ring. Instantly a soft pop sounds then only silence.

Liz feels heavy footsteps come around the kitchen counter and stop next to where she lies. Bob's voice asks, "Liz? Are you all right?"

"Yes Bob. I'm just too weak to stand and I think I wet my pants."

Chuckles of relief come from around the room as strong hands help her up. She looks up and gives Bob a weak smile of thanks. Near the slider door stand two men and a woman. Bob motions for them to come to the dining table then points at the floor. As he walks Liz around the edges of the room to Peter's office she looks down only once at where Alex's body lies with her long gun beside her.

"Did you kill her?"

"No we hit her legs to take her down. She put the last bullet in herself."

"She knew you were close yet she shot to kill me. Why?"

"You knew her too well. Got closer to her than anyone before and then you betrayed her. Her type doesn't want anyone knowing them that well. We got the man in her house as soon as she left for here and other agents caught a woman at the border with phony passports and tickets to some other country. Stay here in Peter's office until I come get you."

Stepping out the office door he gives orders to the other three. "File the body. I'll clean up the table and meet you back in Seattle by twenty-two hundred. We're done here."

Bob quickly stuffs the photos and passports into the manila envelope before coming back to where Liz sits at Peter's desk. He studies her for several seconds without a word he rechecks each desk drawer. Still he says nothing to her. Shaking his head he picks up the manila envelope and smiles down at Liz. "Can you come to Seattle in a few days Liz? The chairman wants to meet you. You can dispose of the furniture or anything else you don't need or want. When can you come?

"Next week? There're things I need to do here. To be honest Bob I want time alone to think."

"Fair enough just make it sooner than later. We didn't know Peter had made up the many passport and money packets we found in the manila envelopes. He may have seen them as his way out. Don't know why he thought that but he must have. We also found several accounts in banks around the world. We're not certain who they belong to, him or the company. I don't, do you?"

"No the only accounts we have are with our financial advisor where we had our stock and there's a checking account at the bank. I'm stunned. I don't know what to think."

Silently the three people walk past the office door carrying a body bag. Liz looks at the floor until she hears the front door close. Then she follows Bob into the hallway. At the front door, she watches the three slip the body bag into the back of a black van and Liz shudders. "Poor Alex she must have been a very lonely person."

"Yeah aren't we all? Don't feel sorry for her Liz. She chose her lifestyle and she wanted to kill you. What we need to find out is how many assassinations around the world in the past twenty years were hers. It's going to be a hell of a job. We haven't found any of her records yet."

CHAPTER NINETEEN

JUNE 19th

BETH

BETH scours the dunes for items lost in the storm one last time then jogs back to the cabin. As she runs she notices the waves are depositing less flotsam than before. Each successive tidal change pushes the storm's litter further south to other beaches crushing the flimsiest items into pulp which mixes with the wave-pounded sand. Some debris is caught and held by masses of bulbous-ended kelp wrapped around float logs that float in and out with each tide.

She is on the steps to her deck when she hears the phone ringing and in her hurry to unlock the slider door she fumbles and drops the key. By the time she opens the door the ringing has stopped. Picking up the receiver she hears the beep of her message service and sees that there are three messages. The first is from the wharf-builder to remind her he will be at the cabin at eight tomorrow morning to finish the last of the dunes near the red cliffs. The second call is from her sister Dana who demands that Beth send her daughter Nicole home as she is a sick girl. The third message is from Nicole who must talk to Aunt Beth about some very important things and will be at the cabin by five.

Beth hangs up the phone and thinks about the messages. *Obviously Dana has gone on one of her rants again. I wonder what she has done to bring Nicole way out here to talk to me. I think I've had a total of an hour with this child since she was born.*

Beth pours a glass of milk and makes a tuna sandwich for her dinner. In the background she hears a soft tapping and stops to listen. She goes to the each door and sees no one. She goes back to the dining table she eats her sandwich. Suddenly someone exclaims, "Yummy."

Nearly choking on a bite Beth stammers, "Liz is that you? Are you here at the table?" When there is no answer Beth finishes the sandwich then washes the empty plate at the sink. Then she hears a loud tapping and turns to see her niece Nicole peering through the glass slider and waving at her. Seeing Beth's surprised look, the young woman shouts, "Aunt Beth it's me Nicole!"

Opening the door Beth exclaims, "Nicole! Come in girl. What are you doing out here? I just heard your message. There's one from your mom too. What's going on? Why are you out here? Come and sit at the table. Have you eaten? No? Sit down and I'll make you a sandwich. Tuna okay? Would you like a cola or water?"

"Yes to both Aunt Beth. I'm starved. Thanks," Nicole answers with a smile as she sits at the table with straight-backed formality.

Beth quickly gets two colas from the fridge and sets one in front of the young woman. Then she pops the lid on her own and takes a large gulp. She hurries back into the kitchen and soon returns with a large tuna sandwich in front of Nicole. "Eat up there're more if you want it."

Nicole opens her mouth to speak.

"No, eat first then we'll talk."

Sipping her cola as she watches the young woman stuff the food into her mouth and chew without modesty Beth wonders why Dana's daughter would show up on her doorstep. *What do I know really know about this child? She is more a stranger than a relative. Dana made sure of that. How did the girl get so brave as to come here to me? Dana must have done something horrid to cause her own daughter to flee from her to me.*

When Nicole is done she takes the empty dishes to the kitchen. There she rinses the glass and fills it with water. Then she drinks it down in four large gulps and sighs. "Thank you so much Aunt Beth. It's been a while since I've eaten. Do you have any cookies or something sweet? I always like to finish my meals with a little sweet." Catching the sound of her own voice Nicole blushes. "I'm so sorry. I sounded just like my mom didn't I? I'm being too presumptuous having dropped in unannounced then asking for more food."

Beth laughs. "Trust me Nicole from the little I know of you you're more like your father. As it so happens I always make a batch of brownies weekly to keep my chocolate fix happy. How about a couple with a glass of milk? Would that do you?"

"Absolute!" Nicole exclaims as a smile spreads over her pretty face. When Beth hands her the plate of sweets she bites into one with great enthusiasm sipping the milk as she chews. "OK, kiddo. Take your time and tell me what is going on with you and your mother," Beth asks noting the surprised look that crosses Nicole's face. "There was a message from Dana right before yours which told me nothing yet said a whole lot. You two must have had quite a row."

"Yeah it was a dilly. She always rags on my choice of classes ever since I decided to become a doctor. Getting a medical degree takes many years of schooling she wants grandchildren now. She nags me all the time to meet some guy who'll make me pregnant and rich and her proud. My sister Nancy did just that by marrying her history professor this spring after he got her pregnant. They eloped and the baby's due this month. Mom tells people they eloped a year ago. Hell Aunt Beth they didn't know each other till last fall. Must admit though the guy's a hunk and he does love Nancy so things are cool that way. Mom's got another generation coming and a professor son-in-law to brag on.

"Last week Nancy told me they plan to move back east as soon as the baby comes. Her hubby has accepted a job as dean of students for some college in New Hampshire. It's as far away from Mom as Nancy can get. I panicked Aunt Beth. I decided to tell Mom my deepest secret the one she never ever thought could possibly ever happen. I simply blurted it out. I told her, 'Mom I'm a lesbian.'"

Beth chuckled. "No wonder I got the call of wrath from Dana. She knew you would head this way. Is what you say true Nicole? Be honest with me. Are you sure you're a lesbian or are you just wanting to shock your mother? Don't play with me. That is one thing I will not tolerate. If you are messing with her to hurt her and using that to do it I will not tolerate it.

However if you truly feel this and have decided to face the reality of coming out to your parents and friends I will stand beside you. If you are the next few months and years will be a hard adjustment. It's not an easy road to walk down Nicole. A lot of gays never make the trip. They play the straight game for years then hit the wall of self-contempt and leave wives, husbands, and children completely hurt and dazed when they finally make their decision. Some others choose suicide rather than make the choice you are."

"Aunt Beth I've known I wasn't like Nancy for almost as long as I have lived. She is the one who told me who I am. She is the best sister and friend anyone could have. I'll miss her terribly when she moves away. But it's final. I moved into an apartment in the University District two days ago. I have an internship that pays a fair salary and will help with costs. I told Dad I was lesbian several years ago and he has backed me totally by keeping my secret from Mom." Taking a deep breath Nicole asks, "Could I please stay here with you tonight Aunt Beth?"

"Of course you may Nicole. Stay as long as you wish. But you must let your parents know you are all right. At least call your father. Tell him I will help you any way I can and that includes help with medical school costs. Give your mom time. She is shocked and hurt. Most parents of gays decide their love for their child is stronger than any disappointment they think their child may have caused them. Your dad obviously loves you. Your mom may do the same. Tell me how did you and your mom end things the other day?"

"She shouted that I was no longer her child and stormed up the stairs to her room. I followed her and tried to talk to her. She wouldn't. I left. Took everything I own including my cat in her carrier. I couldn't leave sweet Dandy-lion to that wicked witch could I?" A crooked smile slips across Nicole's face as she begins to cry. "Aunt Beth it was so awful. I love my mom and now she hates me. I need a place to leave Dandy-lion. Could I leave her here for a while? I can't have her at the apartment and she's such a good cat. I'll take her back when I can. I don't want to lose her too. Could she stay with you a few months?"

Beth laughs with delight. "You know what Nicole? I was just telling a friend that I needed to get me a pet. Yes I'll take

Dandy-lion for as long as you like. I warn you though she may want to stay forever once she sees what a lovely sandbox the beach is. Is she out in your car?"

Nicole nods.

"Why don't you bring her inside?"

"Thank you Aunt Beth thank you so much! You don't know what it means to hear you say you'll take Dandy-lion and stand by me. I've felt so alone and scared since Mom turned her back on me. You'll like Dandy. I have her bed and litter box in the car."

"Your grandmother and grandfather were so opposite of Dana," Beth tells the young woman. "They would have loved you just as they did me when I told them I was a lesbian. Dad simply told me to stand tall and be proud. They never once said anything negative. When I brought Maxine home to meet them they loved her at once because she loved me. Let's give Dana time. She could surprise us and turn out to be the good witch after all.

"Now go get Dandy. Then take one of the jackets from the pegs in the hall and go out on the beach. Walk to the red cliffs. That always clears my mind. We'll talk more later on. I'll call Dana and let her know you're here and safe."

"OK Aunt Beth. I'd like her to know I'm safe. Thanks for loaning me a jacket. All I brought is that black leather coat and it's starting to rain," Nicole says as she runs to get the carrier with Dandy-lion out of the car.

Setting the litter box in the guest room and the food and water dishes in the kitchen Nicole opens the carrier door to let the cat decide when to come out. Then she puts on the thickest jacket hanging on the pegs and heads out onto the beach.

BETH

Picking up the phone Beth watches the girl run north along the waves as she dials Dana. The voice that answers sounds hoarse with exhaustion. "Yes? Who is this?"

"Dana?"

"Beth? Is that you?"

"Yes. I want to let you know Nicole came here a few minutes ago and will stay over night. It seems she has moved to an apartment in Seattle and will go to med school at the University of Washington. I will give her a message to call you if you wish. She is out on the beach right now."

"No. I no longer have children. My daughters are dead to me. Nicole declared herself to be the same sort of deviant as you and Maxine are and Nancy is leaving me for the East Coast. I will never see either of them again. No. I have no message for Nicole. You win Beth. You win. You can have Nicole. I never want to see her again."

"Dana stop talking like that. You can't mean what you are saying. How can you be so stupid? Nicole brought her cat to me to care for while she is in med school and Nancy is moving with her husband to where he has a new position. You know you love them and they love you. What does their father say about what you are doing to them?"

"I'm leaving that son of a bitch. He screamed at me that I was wrong to turn away from Nicole and that I need to let the girls live their lives as they want not the plans I've made to get them to their best possible places in life. He's wrong. You are wrong. You were always against me and so sure you are right. You hated me for years. You'll see though come judgment day. You'll see. All of you will see the truth when I am saved and you all burn in hell. You hear me Beth? You'll burn in hell."

Before Beth can answer the phone goes dead. She sets it on the counter and walks to the dining table. Sitting on one of the chairs she cradles her head in her hands as she realizes the child who came to her today will need her loving support more than ever. Something tickles the calves of her legs and she looks down to see the cat with its back arched and its up-in-the-air hello tail. She leans over and lets her fingers trail along the buff-colored softness as it circles her legs and looks up with golden eyes and soft mews. Picking it up in her arms, she whispers, "Dandy did you hear? Dana's children have turned on her. She no longer controls their lives. They have escaped just as I always hoped they would. Now they have a chance for good lives. Nicole has you and me and we must help her and love her. This will be her home and you'll be here to greet her every time she comes for a visit.

"Maxine, now I understand what you meant by my saving two small lives. Maybe even help a sister back to wellness if Dana will let me. If only she will listen to reason while her children can still forgive her. Oh Dandy, it's such a sad thing."

Hearing running footsteps Beth turns to see Nicole hurry along the north deck to the front of the cabin. Taking the cat with her Beth opens the front door and calls, "Nicole can I help you with anything?"

"That's alright Aunt Beth. I just have a backpack with a few things in it. All my other stuff is at the apartment. That's why I didn't come sooner." As she talks she grabs a pack from the back of the car and swings it over her shoulders. Then she slams the car door and locks it. Walking to where Beth stands hugging Dandy Nicole smiles. "Thanks for the beach time Aunt Beth. You were right. A hike on the beach is great think time." Scratching behind the cat's ears she sighs. "You're going to love living here Dandy."

"Glad it worked for you. By the way I got hold of your mother and yes she is the most stupid person I have ever known.

Seems your father has moved out over how she handled your announcement. From what I could tell over the phone Dana is in one of her deeply depressed cycles. Does she ever stay on her meds?"

"Mother needs nothing, Aunt Beth. Don't you know that? Meds, bite your tongue!" Nicole laughs with disgust. "Don't you realize it's all of us who are sick? Don't you know we're to kowtow to her every whim? Dance to her ranting and raving? Dear God can you even guess how wonderful it is to have survived to be twenty-one and move out of her house? Good for Dad I say. Now maybe he'll have some happy years. He is the only reason Nancy and I grew up the least bit normal." Nicole chuckles as she takes Dandy from Beth and kisses the cat's brow.

Tossing her head Beth roars with delight startling the cat who jumps from Nicole's arms and flees under the sofa. The two women watch open mouthed for several seconds before Nicole drops her pack wraps her arms around the older woman and hugs her tightly. "Thank you so much Aunt Beth! Thank you!"

Hugging her niece Beth rocks back and forth spinning them both in the joyous moment. Then Beth picks up Nicole's backpack and opens the guestroom door. "This is your room from now on Nicole so make yourself at home. There are towels and toiletries in the bathroom. Take a long hot shower and get into your cozies. There are more brownies and milk if you're still hungry. Better yet go crawl into bed if you need to. You've had a big day and tomorrow will come early if you plan to be back at the U by noon. So bathe and bed. I'll wake you for a very early breakfast and send off. This is your home with a capital H from now on. OK, kiddo?"

Her face rosy from the beach walk and finding a safe harbor in the midst of her life's worst storm Nicole can only nod.

CHAPTER TWENTY

JUNE 19th

ELIZA

ELIZA pours a tall glass of iced tea and adds two shots of Irish whiskey to it then takes it out to the chaise lounge on the deck to watch the sunset. Letting the cold drink settle her shakes she scans the beach scene below her deck and ponders over the last few weeks. *Time will tell if I've gotten away with killing Jack. I was lucky Penny told me Mike was in my house a long time before I got back from my run. I could have hung myself. I always think aloud when working things out. And I have a lot to work out. It would help to be with the other women I see in my home. They were at the tables again this morning and I did everything except stand on my head to get them to see me. Maybe this is the consequence for my sins this seeing my others yet being unable to reach them for the rest of my life. I wish I felt more guilt but I only feel remorse. Jack deserved to be shot and I don't feel guilty about doing it. In so many ways I would never have cared about him and Peg. That day without my meds Jack's past came at me like a locomotive and knocked* *me askew. I felt so violated that to be rid of him seemed the only solution. Peg though not her. Peg was my best friend for so many years. I wish it hadn't been Peg. I would love to talk to her about all that has happened. I'm so alone and I miss her. Thank heavens I have Dana and her twins.*

Suddenly Eliza shakes her head and snorts in disgust. "What the hell are you doing Eliza? Huh? What sort of pity pit are you throwing yourself into Elizabeth Ann Anderson now known as Eliza Staples? What do you really have to be moaning about?" Eliza laughs aloud and drinks the last of her spiked tea. "You are wonderful and you are loved. I repeat Eliza Staples is loved." As she talks to herself her others come into her thoughts. "Tonight is the summer solstice's eve and I am sure they will be at their tables and I will meet them tonight."

Excited by this realization Eliza takes her empty glass into the house and refills it then scans the room for her others. Suddenly very unsettled at not seeing them as well as not knowing if she found all the hidden 'bugs' she shouts, "Damn you both. Where the hell are you?" Then she thinks, *If only I were sure those bugs were gone. I need some way to find out if I found them all. There's only one way to find out for sure and that's to proposition asshole Sheriff Frank Gilbert.* At the thought she laughs and shouts, "I wonder what Frank Gilbert would say if I told him how horny he makes me. Would he come here tonight? Will he make passionate love to me till neither of us can walk? How will I have the courage to tell him?"

As her words ring through the rooms Eliza realizes she may have opened a can of worms she doesn't want to deal with. *If there are any bugs left in here I'll soon know. Frank is as big a womanizer as Jack ever was. He won't pass up an opportunity like this no matter what he says about being a loving and faithful husband. If he hears what I just said he'll be here by tomorrow. Hell he'll be here tonight.*

CHAPTER TWENTY-ONE

JUNE 20th

TOGETHER

LIZ wakes before dawn and sees stars twinkle in a clear sky through her bedroom window. Immediately she sits up. "It's the summer solstice!" she exclaims before rushing into the shower. Within minutes she is dressed and turning the knob to her bedroom door. As she pulls it open her movements seem to shift into slow motion then suddenly she is propelled through the doorway and smacks into a startled Beth. Both women are so surprised to see their other in her home that for several seconds they only stare at each other not sure if what they see is real.

Then Beth reaches for Liz and wraps her arms around her. "Liz it *is* you! You're in my home or am I in yours? I never expected this."

Wide eyed with joy Liz returns the hug as she stammers, "Neither did I Beth. Isn't it amazing?"

"It sure is." Beth answers as she looks around the space. "Look how my cabin settles right into yours and we're together without those sparks flashing around us! Isn't it wonderful?"

"Yes. Yes it's wonderfully amazing and phenomenal." Liz laughs as she hugs Beth. "What a special day this solstice is going to be. Do you suppose Eliza Staples is going to be with us?" Both turn to the dining tables. Eliza is nowhere to be seen though her first floor is in full view.

"Look at this Liz." Beth points around her. "Did you see how my cabin meshes into yours and yours into Eliza's? Isn't it amazing?"

Liz laughs. "Yes it looks as if they were made as a set with the smaller fitting into the larger like measuring cups."

Beth walks to her kitchen sink and is stopped by her counter though she can still see the two other homes. "I'm stopped by my own counter yet I can see both your home and the other home through the walls of your home. Do you see what I mean? Can you come into mine?"

"Yes I can," yelps Liz her heart pounding with excitement as she moves about Beth's rooms as the cabin meshes with her own. "Look I can go right through your walls but am stopped from going into Eliza's home by my own walls. Gosh Beth it's so amazing to be in Dad's old cabin again. I know you've done new work on the uphill side but these front rooms are the same and it's as if I've stepped back in time. I wish Eliza were with us. It would be wonderful to have her here. Maybe she'll come later in the day."

"Liz look, Eliza is at her table. Eliza can you hear me?" Beth asks as both women rush to sit on the chairs on either side of their other. Beth touches the woman's hand asking, "You're Eliza Staples aren't you? I'm Beth Anderson. This is Liz Day who you met a few weeks ago. Will you please stay and talk with us? Eliza? You and Liz and I are from one life. At least that's what we've come to believe. We want to know you. Please stay here and talk with us."

Eliza stares at each face beside her for many seconds before she reacts. Then without a word she wraps her arms around each woman and her tears answer for her. They in turn hold onto her until her sobs turn to laughter. Surprised by Eliza's response Beth asks anxiously. "Liz do you think we've driven Eliza over the brink?"

Eliza exclaims. "No Beth I'm fine. Please sit here and hold my hand until I can pull myself together. I need to feel you both to know I'm finally with you and not having hallucinations. I was so afraid you two wouldn't come through to me and I'd always be the one watching from the other side. Please stay with me longer."

Liz assures her, "We need to feel your hand in ours too Eliza. We need know we're together as we were years ago when we were one entity named Elizabeth Ann Anderson. Isn't that right Beth?" Choked with emotions Beth can only nod and hold onto the hands of her others.

Liz continues to speak to Eliza. "Believe me when I say we are both of you and of each other as you are of us. Somehow we came together at this time. Neither Beth nor I are sure how it happened. We think it was the trauma of losing our loved ones on the first of June. We really don't know. Only God knows how we happened and we can only rejoice in being together. Will you try to stay and be with us? We'd like you to be part of our lives. Do you understand Eliza?"

Taking a deep shuddering breath Eliza smiles widely and her eyes are lit with joy. "Yes Elizabeth Ann Anderson I understand this whole thing. I've sat at these tables and watched you both for two weeks and tried everything to get your attention. After rejecting you so soundly that first day I thought you would never notice me again. I have sat next to you both many times talking at you. My touch only caused you to disappear. Nothing worked. I wondered if I'd ever meet you again.

"Since this is the summer solstice I had high hopes I'd see you this morning. I came down to the table an hour ago but neither of you was here. I was so disappointed and so afraid you were lost to me even though I could see both your homes sitting within my own. Then poof you both walk right up to me out of nowhere. How did you do that?"

Shaking her head Beth laughs, "We don't know Eliza. It just happens. Liz and I smacked into each other at our bedroom doors. Liz told you that we lost our loved ones on the same day each about two in the afternoon. We think those traumas created such energy around us that our dimensions opened to our others. We believe the three of us are parallel lives of the same child who spent her summers here at Redcliff's Beach in her father's cabin. The solstice is one of the days when planets aligning with the sun and moon pull apart like dimensions to their others. This had to be the day you would come through to us as we are of each other. When we hear your story maybe we'll understand why it took so long to meet you."

Beth takes a deep breath before she continues, "Liz and I know that our lives were the exactly the same up to when we were fourteen. At that time there was a traffic accident that killed her parents and sister who was named Dana. On that same date my family was in a fender bender which only injured my sister Dana as she did not wear her seatbelt. My parents lived many years afterward. My father was killed by a mugger and my mother died just five years ago.

"You've seen how our houses have arranged the smaller into the larger. My cabin is nearly the same as the original Anderson cabin. Maxine and I added on a carport and guestroom and enlarged the bathroom but it still fits easily into Liz's expanded home and hers fits into your large elegant house. Though I see all of your homes around my cabin I can only walk within my own home. It is the same with Liz. Though she can move through my cabin rooms she is limited to her own home. Whereas your home is so large you could walk through both our houses without being stopped. You must have a big family to need so much space."

Beth's last statement makes Eliza blush then laugh at her own embarrassment. "No I don't Beth. It's my gift to me for living with an asshole of a husband for so many years. We had no children. My sister Dana and I planned the house to include two large master suites for the both of us along with smaller suites for her twin daughters. The rooms on this level will be shared by all. Dana will move here next month now that her house has sold. Her twins Janice and Julia will visit toward the end of summer."

Eliza smiles at the other women as she continues, "I am so very happy to be with you both. Could we stay here and talk? I want to tell you my story and it will take a while. Then I want to know everything about you both." Eliza pauses. "Be forewarned that my story may shock you. But you mustn't turn away from me. You can't. Promise me you'll try to understand why I did what I did and stay with me even after I've told you all of it."

Liz and Beth promise Eliza and for the next six hours the three women share their life stories including the deaths of loved ones and their plans for their futures. When the anniversary clock on Liz's fireplace chimes three the women are brought back to the present. Their smiles reflect the comfort and sense of peace they feel being with each other.

Liz stands and stretches. "My head is full of cobwebs and whirling with the fact that Eliza stayed in Hood River all her life. That would explain why she didn't come through to us as quickly as we did each other. Eliza you must be the original Elizabeth Ann Anderson and the two of us split from you. That day you said your dad died is the same day our dad moved us to Seattle. After that Beth and I have the same memories of those years following until the horrible car accident that changed our lives forever. We feel this is also the trauma which caused our lives to split from each other."

Nodding Beth agrees. "We were each ten years old on the day Eliza's dad died and ours moved us from Hood River. All our memories are the same until the accident that killed Liz's family and injured my sister Dana. We were fourteen. You said you were that age when your mother married her new husband and moved you to Portland. Is that right Eliza?"

"Yes it is. But my head is too full and aching." Eliza laughs. "Let's stop for a while as my brain needs a breather. Let's go to the beach and race to our touchstone and celebrate the solstice."

"Let's do it." Liz exclaims as she turns towards her slider door. "Let's go slap our touchstone together. Remember if we get separated come back home and sit at the tables. Agreed?"

"Agreed." Beth and Eliza shout as they follow Liz to their own doors and start to go outside. At that instant three things happen, one to each woman.

To Liz the kitchen phone rings.

To Beth someone pounds on her front door.

To Eliza the front doorbell chimes.

CHAPTER TWENTY-TWO

JUNE 20th

LIZ

LIZ is in the open door to her deck when her phone rings. Instinctively she turns and hurries to answer it. It is Bob Drake. "Don't talk," he barks. "Go in Peter's office close the door and lock it with the deadbolt. Punch the red button on the right side of the desk. More of Alex's people have been spotted on Shoreline Drive. They'll be at your drive within minutes. Don't hang up, go now!"

On pure instinct to survive Liz drops the phone and runs to the office door. Quickly opening it and pushing inside she bolts the door twice behind her. Taking the distance to the desk in two leaps she hits the red button on Peter's desk. Her actions take only a few seconds yet it seems much longer. Throwing herself into the far corner of Peter's office, she hunkers down letting the desk shield her from whatever comes through the door. Her heart pounds so loud in her ears it masks any sounds from outside the door. Forcing herself to take deep breaths she slowly manages to calm herself and scans the room for alternate exits in case something happens to Bob. Then she sees the door to Peter's bathroom and suddenly needs to use it. Taking off her sandals she rises from the floor and silently pads to the door. Trying the knob she finds it locked and tries it again. When it doesn't open she realizes she is trapped. There are no other escape routes. Sudden fear overwhelms her and she runs back to the corner where she'd sat.

This is what Bob meant when he said Peter's office was secure from outside entry. A safe room he called it. I didn't understand. Now I do. Peter needed this room for protection from some unknown intruder who wanted what he knew. Now I know that someone is Alex. No wonder she tried to kill me.

Suddenly furious Liz hisses, "Damn you Peter Day damn you. Did your life have anything to do with me? What really went on in this room all those years we were together? Where the hell was my head? Why didn't I question the locks on this room? Did I really think it was for protection against industrial espionage to your company? That's the biggest joke of all as you never owned a company! Did I ever think I might be the one who had to use it because of your 'business' actions?" Liz is so angry she spits the last words. "Damn you Peter if I don't live through this I'm going to wring your neck when I see you. Eliza and Beth will be at the rock wondering where I am. You bastard you better make certain I live through this to see my others again."

As if in answer a loud rapping comes from the door and Liz instinctively opens her mouth to respond then shuts it immediately. She knows it isn't Bob as he would call her by name. Someone else is out there someone looking for her. Then a woman's voice calls sweetly to her, "Hello in here. Hello? All is well. You can come out now. It's all right. Unlock the door and come out. We need you to identify the body we have found."

When Liz doesn't answer the voice becomes harsh. "Open this door now and come out. There's no other way out." When she doesn't answer there is a long pause. Then the woman calls sweetly to her again. "Hello? Open the door Mrs. Day? Peter is here and I will kill him if you don't unlock this door. Open this door and he will live."

For a second the words about Peter startle Liz until she remembers Peter is now part of the ocean. Clenching her teeth so she won't snap back an angry answer she crawls under Peter's desk and pulls her knees up to her chin. As she does a peaceful warmth flows through her and she knows she is where she should be. She is safe.

Sudden pounding on the door startles her and a man's gruff voice demands she open the door. He shouts obscenities as he continues to pound the door so hard she feels the vibration in the floor with each blow. Suddenly the pounding stops and Liz hears voices shouting and several gunshots being fired. Then there is only silence the same eerie silence that came after the shooting of Alexandria Petrow.

Liz crawls out from under the desk and stretches before she sinks into the leather desk chair and waits. Sitting in Peter's chair gives her comfort and helps calm her. She is certain Bob Drake will come to her only when it is completely safe for her to unlock the door if he lives.

Nearly an hour later she hears his voice. "Liz? Bob Drake. Are you all right? Don't open the door. We have cleanup to do and it'll be best if you stay in there till it's done. I'll get back to you soon. Liz? You hear me?"

"Yes Bob I hear you," she calls out shivering for she knows his meaning of "cleanup." Feeling nauseous she pushes herself out of the chair and hurries to the bathroom door. This time the knob turns and she rushes in to use the toilet.

CHAPTER TWENTY-THREE

JUNE 20th

BETH

BETH'S response to the knocking at her door is immediate. Thinking that Nicole has returned she rushes through the cabin and opens the door. Expecting to see her niece she is stunned to find Dana standing in front of her.

Her sister's face twists with rage and she holds a large pistol pointed directly at Beth. "You damned bitching queer I'm going to kill you!" She yells at Beth as she levels the gun and pulls the trigger five times.

Even before Dana yells Beth Instinctively turns off to the side letting two bullets tear into her left shoulder and arm. The force spins her backward into the hallway and she lands face down. She doesn't see Dana continue to aim wildly and shoot three more times. Two of these bullets miss Beth. The third hits high on the backside of Beth's left leg. Beth doesn't feel the impact as darkness finds her first and she sinks into its comfort.

As she drifts above her body Maxine comes to her. *Go back Beth. Your time is not yet. Go back darling. You have a life yet to live. Others need you. Go back.* Through a gray haze Beth crawls toward the dining table as she prays that Liz and Eliza return from the beach. *They'll find me. Send help. Dana's gone. I live. I still live. Damn bitch damn bitch.*

CHAPTER TWENTY-FOUR

JUNE 20th

ELIZA

ELIZA ignores the doorbell to make certain she doesn't lose contact with her others and closes the French door before racing down the steps to the beach path. She hears her name shouted as well as pounding footsteps along the side deck coming from the front of her house. Giving a quick glance over her shoulder Eliza sees Mike Hartman running at her with a gun in his right hand. His face is twisted with anger as he leaps over the railing onto a sand dune shooting as he does.

Instinctively Eliza throws herself to one side of the path and runs through the grass-topped dunes not stopping even when she reaches the hard-packed sand near the tide line. Her focus is on the red cliffs to the north. She takes no notice of the groups on the beach: volley ball games, kiting groups, or families sprawled on patches of sun-heated sand; all those people now looking toward the house where the shots came from. Eliza only knows that to stop is to die so she runs without looking back. "If this is my last day I will end it at my touchstone with my others at the base of the red cliffs."

She repeats these words until she reaches the slab of stone at the base of the cliffs. Staggering onto it she slaps the large red stone in the vertical cliff and cries out, "This run is good and done. Liz? Beth? I'm here. It's Eliza. Beth? Liz? Are you here? Where are you?"

Realizing her others are not coming through to her Eliza scans the area by the cliffs for them. They are nowhere near the red cliffs. Looking back towards her home three miles away she realizes there is no one running toward her. The beach is crowded but Mike Hartman is nowhere to be seen. "What the hell happened back there? Was Mike really there? Did I actually see him shoot at me? What's that movement around my house?"

Then she sees a white car emerge from the public entrance to this end of the beach. It moves slowly through the crowds with its band of red and blue lights flashing. When it reaches the hard packed sand near the wave line it picks up speed. The back of Eliza's neck tingles as it moves closer. Waiting on the edge of the slab of stone Eliza watches it stop fifty feet from where she sits. The car's passenger door opens and Frank Gilbert steps out and walks up to her. Tears drop onto her cheeks as he tells her, "You can come home Eliza. It's safe. Mike is gone. The son of a bitch got himself drunk last night in Hood River and bragged he was coming here to kill you. Luckily someone called me so I had time to contact the local sheriff to watch for him. The county's helicopter flew me over. Deputy Browne here got me to your place as fast as he could. We knew where he was most of the time. However we needed him to make his move before we could pick him up. They saw him drive past your drive earlier this morning. Must have left his car up the road and doubled back on foot through the dunes.

"The deputy was briefing me when we heard him shout then shoot at you. He shot six times. Thank God you were both running when he did. Otherwise he'd have got you. He chased you into the dunes all the while yelling he'd kill you too just like Jack and Peg got it. Even after the deputy shot him in the leg he yelled that he killed you too.

"I'm sorry I didn't believe you before Eliza. Hate to tell you I thought it was you who killed Jack and Peg or at least had something to do with it. Almost got you killed with my stupidity. Yeah it was me killed Mike wouldn't put down his gun after the deputy put a bullet in his damn leg. When Mike shot back at the deputy I shot to kill him."

Eliza listens to him. Then without a word she slips off the edge of the stone and walks past the police car for several yards before racing down the beach to her home. By the time she gets there one ambulance is leaving while the team from a second one waits to make certain she is uninjured.

While they are checking her over Frank Gilbert comes into the house and silently watches. Eliza doesn't acknowledge his presence by either word or gesture. She knows what he wants. She doesn't. After the medics leave Frank walks towards her with his arms open to embrace her. Eliza holds up both hands and shakes her head violently. He stops. Making certain her meaning is clear Eliza hurries past him and opens the front door then waits for him to leave. When he walks past her to the patrol car she quickly shuts the door and bolts it.

Running up the stairs to the widows walk Eliza watches the ambulance and the police cars drive south along Shoreline Drive. Then she goes down to her bedroom strips off her clothes and steps into the shower. In the middle of the shower's back teal green tiled wall is a large tile with a deep red handprint. Without hesitation she slaps it and shouts, "I declare this run good and done!"

CHAPTER TWENTY-FIVE

JUNE 20th

ENDINGS

LIZ realizes she is holding her breath when she hears Bob's voice telling her to open the door. She does and steps into the hallway. There are no signs of struggle though the hallway tiles are damp. "No tell-tale signs left behind?" Liz says gesturing at the wet floor as she walks out the front door with Bob trailing after her.

"Not if we have time," he says smiling in an attempt at covering the frown that slips across his brow. "Liz this is a need to know event. Understand?"

"Of course Bob. I've only my others to tell anyway and as you so firmly told me they only exist in my head. Besides I don't need to be told that. You and Peter could have trusted me more. Maybe then he'd still be alive and Alex would have moved years ago. I've a lot of thinking to do. Who do I trust? I'm in a void that needs answers." Seeing the look in his eyes she shakes her head, "Not from you."

"I didn't intend to try," he snaps back as he walks to the car waiting for him. When he opens the door he turns and tells her. "I'll be in touch next week Liz. Call if you need anything sooner anything at all." Returning his smile she waves as the car slips onto Shoreline Drive.

As Liz walks through her entry the light deepens to a reddish gold. Suddenly she is in the old family cabin and nearly trips over Beth who is sprawled on the floor in front of her. Falling to her knees Liz shouts, "Beth, Beth! What happened? What? Oh my God! You've been shot. Beth? Who shot you?"

Beth moans as her eyes crack open. "Dana. Dana. Get my phone call nine-one-one. Liz?"

Liz looks around frantically. "Where's your phone?"

Beth hisses, "Kitchen," then goes limp.

Liz scurries to the kitchen sees Beth's phone and dials 911 on it. In seconds a dispatcher answers and she screams, "I'm shot! I'm shot. Help me. Help me!" When asked who is calling Liz screams, "Beth Anderson! Beth Anderson. I'm at Redcliff's Beach. Only cabin here. Help me. I'm bleeding to death! Help me."

To the question of who shot her Liz screams, "My sister Dana! My sister Dana shot me. Help me." Told to leave the phone on Liz rushes to Beth's side and lays it beside one of her hands. Into Beth's nearest ear Liz whispers, "They're coming Beth. Hold on. Help will be here soon."

Realizing Beth's wounds are oozing too much blood Liz strips off her own T-shirt and rips it into strips. Lifting Beth's shirt she stuffs strips into the open wounds and presses hard on the leg wound to slow the flow of blood. When she does as much as she can she pulls the throw from the sofa and covers Beth with it. Then she holds one of Beth's hands and waits for the rescue team.

She hears the helicopter long before it lands on the beach below Beth's cabin and Liz runs to the slider door to unlock it. Then she goes into the cabin's kitchen and watches as the rescue team scrambles onto the deck then moves into the cabin. Liz starts to speak to the rescuers but as soon as they step into the room Beth's cabin vanishes. Almost leaping to her own dining table where she knows she can see that portion of Beth's cabin Liz watches the EMTs work over her other. Soon they have Beth fastened into a stretcher cage and carry her out the slider door to the helicopter on the beach.

Rushing to Beth's cabin window Liz sees the helicopter rise off the beach then zip off to the northeast. "Dear God please let them reach the hospital in time. Let Beth live. How will I ever know? There is no way to see her except in this area where our dimensions come together in our homes. Damn! I wish Eliza were here. Where is she? Eliza? Are you home? Are you here?" When there is no answer Liz sighs. "Poor Eliza she must have gone to our touchstone." Looking at her watch she sees that more than three hours have passed. "Damn she must be back by now. Eliza where are you?"

"Liz I'm right behind you. Where did you and Beth go? I ran to the red cliffs and neither of you were there. I've been sitting here at this table for over an hour. Where have you two been? You're not going to believe what happened to me! I had such a scare. When we left to go to the rocks the doorbell rang. Oh hell I can't talk about it now. I'm all done in. Let's have a glass of wine and something to eat. I'll tell you all about it then," Eliza chatters as she disappears into her kitchen.

Liz rushes to her kitchen counter and watches Eliza pour three glasses of wine she shouts, "Eliza, Beth's not here. When you said you were here all that time I thought you saw what happened to her. She was shot by her sister Dana. She lost a lot of blood. I used her phone to call nine-one-one then a helicopter came with a rescue team and took her away. I don't know if she lives or has died. We won't know until she comes home if she ever does. " Suddenly exhausted by all that has happened Liz puts her head in her hands and cries.

Stunned by what Liz tells her Eliza moves quickly to her side and pushes her gently onto one of the dining chairs. "Damn it Liz! Don't you see what happened? Not only did you and Beth get shot at so did I. The guy who killed my husband Jack and friend Peg came here to kill me. He shot several times as I ran through the dunes to the red cliffs. Luckily Sheriff Frank Gilbert followed him and shot him before he shot me."

Liz wipes her eyes as a puzzled look spreads across her face. "Eliza, wasn't the person who killed your husband you? Isn't that what you told Beth and me just this morning?"

"All right it seems Mark did me a great favor by getting himself killed. Everyone heard him scream he was going to kill me too. Frank Gilbert said he shouted it over and over. Even when the local deputy shot him he yelled it. The whole beach crowd heard him. His own words condemned him and his death closed the case very conveniently for me. It's over and I no longer have to worry if there are any more of those damned 'bugs' still in my home."

Seeing the frown on Liz's face Eliza nods. "Yes I know the negative karma is still with me and I've got to atone for my actions. I'll have to do many good things all the rest of my life. I sure don't want that load around my neck when I get to the pearly gates."

"You'd better start making up for your dirty deed real soon." Liz tells her. "Maybe that money I hid can be used to help all three of us. We seem to be very much connected to each other. Any sort of action taken at one seems to rebound onto the others. We can begin as soon as Beth gets back from the hospital. She'll need lots of care and both of us will have to share that with her niece Nicole. Isn't that the girl's name?"

"Yes it is. However it'll be weeks before Beth gets back if she was hurt as badly as you said. I feel awful that she took some of my justice due with those bullets. Her sister Dana must be crazy. It's hard to believe she's of my own Dana. That woman should be in police custody If the sheriff acted quickly. He must have caught her by now. I wish we knew for sure. What else can we do but wait? Liz? I'm starved. How about you? I'm going to fix us a great dinner."

Liz follows Eliza to her own kitchen counter where she watches Eliza pull various items from the refrigerator and cupboards. "If you'll do that in my kitchen, I could help."

CHAPTER TWENTY-SIX

EPILOGUE

AUGUST 1ˢᵗ

LIZ and ELIZA and her sister Dana are together at their joined tables when **BETH'S** cabin reappears within their homes for the first time since the shooting. Both women gasp and rush into the center of the area and wait with great excitement. Suddenly the cabin door opens and Beth's niece Nicole comes in carrying a suitcase and takes it into Beth's bedroom. Then she goes back to open the door wider and asks, "Are you all right Aunt Beth?" The woman she speaks to walks slowly past her using a pair of crutches and answers, "Yes Nicole. I'll be on my sofa. It's so good to be back in my cabin again. Thank you so much for helping me home."

Smiling her answer the young woman vanishes out past her yelling back, "I'll get the boxes from the car. You sit and take it easy. I cleaned the cabin and stocked the kitchen with easy-to-fix meals. You're not to do anything but sit there and let Dandy-lion welcome you home. Do you hear me?"

Still talking to Beth the young woman returns with a box and turns into the bathroom. Then she again disappears out the front door returning with a box filled with cards, gifts, and plants. "I should have brought this one home yesterday," she chatters as she walks across the room to set the box on the kitchen counter. "You were right to leave the candy at the hospital for the nurses. Better they eat it than us. What do you say I take these plants over to that nursing home in Ocean Shores? Then you won't have to water them."

When Beth doesn't answer her Nicole turns toward the sofa and asks, "Aunt Beth? Is anything wrong? Oh you have company! Why didn't you tell me your friends were here? I'm so sorry I yelled so much. Hey! What the hell? Mom! What are you doing here? How did you get out of the sanitarium? Get out of this house right now. Go on out to my car and I'll drive you back. You can't stay here. Damn it Mom haven't you hurt Aunt Beth enough? Do you really think I'd let you hurt her again. Get out of here right now." The young woman screams and advances toward Dana, Eliza's sister sitting near Beth.

Shouting over her niece's rage Beth stands between Nicole and Dana. "Nicole stop. Stop. This isn't your mother. This is Eliza's sister Dana and these are Liz and Beth. All of us are parallel lives of each other. We are each other's other."

"What did you just say Aunt Beth? You said these women are your others and she is my mom's other? Is that what you said? How can they be so much like you and here if I never knew of them? They look exactly like you. What's so funny Aunt Beth?"

"Oh my dear Nicole, I have so much to tell you," Beth answers as she walks to where Nicole stands and gives her a hug. "I'll try to explain."

The End